PUCK GRABBER

PUCK GRABBER

by C. P. *and* O. B. JACKSON

Illustrated by Robert Henneberger

Whittlesey House
McGRAW-HILL BOOK COMPANY, INC.
New York   London   Toronto

Also by C. P. and O. B. Jackson

STAR KICKER

HILLBILLY PITCHER

BASKETBALL CLOWN

And by C. Paul Jackson

ALL-CONFERENCE TACKLE

ROSE BOWL ALL-AMERICAN

DUB HALFBACK

ALL-TOURNAMENT FORWARD

LITTLE LEAGUER'S FIRST UNIFORM

GIANT IN THE MIDGET LEAGUE

SPICE'S FOOTBALL

Library of Congress Catalog Card Number: 57-12583

Published by Whittlesey House
A division of the McGraw-Hill Book Company, Inc.

Contents

CHAPTER 1

Two Problems

There were only fifty or so Northern High students watching the practice hockey game between Meinland High and Northern High. They were a mere handful in spacious Northern Tech Ice Palace, Northern High's home rink. Bill Jones suspected that it was not by chance that the Northern followers gathered in the section of seats behind the Meinland players' box midway of the third period.

He knew that his suspicions were well founded when his line came off the ice.

"That guy who writes sports for the *Northern Star* has rocks in his noggin!" One of the Northern High boys spoke loudly. "Where does he get that stuff about Meinland being a threat to our chances of repeating as Conference champs!"

"Yeah! Meinland couldn't beat a carpet!"

"Our guys are toying with them. Anytime we want a goal, we just swarm in there and get one!"

"Anybody could beat that Meinland goalie!"

"You can say that again. He's worse than a sieve!"

A scowl wrinkled the face of Bill Jones. His

gray eyes were bleak as he looked gloomily at the boy shifting nervously in front of the Meinland goal. It wasn't the needling of Northern High fellows that made him scowl. The trouble was that the crack about Meinland's goalie wasn't so far off.

Pete Tinsley was really having a bad time in the Meinland nets. Words that Coach Le Beau had said just before the practice game started ran through Bill's mind.

". . . Keep after the boys on defense. Tinsley has tried hard and will keep on, but I'm afraid he just doesn't have what it takes to play goal. I'm afraid that we have more of a problem than you realize, Bill . . ."

Bill's scowl deepened. If only Ben Hoad's folks hadn't moved from Meinland. There wouldn't be any needling cracks about Meinland's goalie if Ben were in the nets!

Thinking of the loss of Ben Hoad, three-year veteran goalie, brought Cliff Beardsley to Bill's mind. He looked toward where Beardsley had just outwhacked the Northern center for the puck at a faceoff.

Cliff Beardsley had played hockey on the top line for a crack school team in the East. His father had come to Meinland to fill the position from which Mr. Hoad had been transferred. Cliff

It was a practice game

Beardsley would have been a welcome addition to Meinland hockey if his coming had not meant the loss of Ben Hoad—and if he didn't have such an irritating cockiness. If he—

"Watch it!" Bill's thoughts broke off, and he shouted as Northern intercepted a Beardsley pass. "Back on defense quick!" Bill yelled.

Meinland's defense proved inadequate. The Northern center blazed a hard shot at the corner of the goal cage. Pete Tinsley had been pulled badly out of position. His lunge across the goal mouth was too late. The red light behind the Meinland goal flashed to indicate a Northern score.

"He should have stopped that one," Bill muttered. "He shouldn't have let them sucker him!"

"All right, Bill." Coach Le Beau leaned forward from the end of the bench. "Take your line back out there. Let's see you fellows get that goal back—quick!"

They did not get the goal back quickly. The two minutes or so that Le Beau left his lines on the ice had nearly passed when a Northern defense man took a pass near the boards and darted across the Meinland blue line.

Bill sized up the pattern of attack. He slammed into the puck carrier. The stiff body check jarred the puck from the Northern boy's control. Bill deftly hooked the rubber disk with his stick and his

10

skates bit into the ice in short but swift strokes.

"Rusty! Dick!" Bill yelled at the wings of his line. "Here we go!"

At the edge of his visual field, Bill saw the Northern center skating fast to get in front of Rusty Hanlon, Bill's left wing. Rusty was forced to drag a little to keep onside short of the blue line.

Dick Carney, right wing of the Hanlon-Jones-Carney line, kept the pattern of the play. Dick darted down the right lane toward the goal cage. Rusty bored in from the left. Rusty's pass to Dick was partially deflected by a Northern stick. Dick swept his stick in what appeared to be an angle shot at goal.

The goalie lunged across his crease. Too late he saw that Dick had not shot. Quickly he jabbed his wide stick across the goal mouth. But the split second he had lost ruined his attempt to clear. Bill Jones reached the puck a vital instant ahead of the goalie's stick.

Meinland High's ace center drilled a whistling shot into the left lobe of the goal netting. The red light behind Northern's cage flared bright.

"Goal!" The goal umpire signaled the referee, nodding vigorously. "Good goal!"

"Way to go!" Rusty Hanlon shouted. A wisp of reddish hair sticking between the crosspieces of his head guard rippled as Rusty skated fast to Bill.

11

He clapped Bill on a padded shoulder. "Old play-maker in person! The professionals don't set 'em up and cash 'em any nicer than that one, Bill!"

The referee dug the puck out of the net cords and skated toward center ice for a new faceoff. Five boys piled through the gate to the Meinland players' box. A new front line and replacements at defense. A fresh line and defense men skated from the Northern box. Both coaches were utilizing this practice game to give workouts to as many of their boys as possible.

A slender, blond boy skated past Bill.

"Not bad, that goal," Cliff Beardsley said. "But keep your glimmers open, Jones. Watch how a real center outslickers their defense!"

Bill just stared. There was that irritating cockiness again.

"Well, that ties it all up," Dick Carney said as they skated to the players' box. His dark eyes gleamed. "Four light-blinkers we've cashed. Our old production line is going to produce better than ever this year!"

"You can say that nine times!" Rusty nodded. "If the second line can just hold Northern, we'll show the hot shot champs they'll have competition this year!"

Bill said nothing. An uneasy thought nagged increasingly at the back of his mind. No matter

12

how many goals they produced, it was no good if the other team scored more. He loosened the chin strap and removed his padded head guard.

Sweat made his dark-brown hair glisten almost black. Bill slid along the bench toward the man standing at the end. Bill looked at Coach Le Beau.

The coach met Bill's gaze. His eyes were the same clear gray as Bill's. His face was full and round. His body was rounder than one would expect a man of his slightly below-average height to have.

"Smooth play," Le Beau said. "Four goals is about as much as a coach could ask from a line."

Bill had a feeling that the coach had left unsaid more than he'd said. Le Beau looked out over the rink. Bill's gaze followed. The coach was eyeing the Meinland goalie.

Pete Tinsley moved restlessly across his crease. Bill frowned. Pete was too tense. Why the heck couldn't Pete relax?

Bill glanced at the coach. Le Beau's round face held a sober expression. Bill's frown deepened. *Okay, so Pete's allowed four goals. And he was badly fooled on three of them.* Bill did not say the words aloud. *Pete's bound to develop. Anyway, why should Coach get the idea that I'd do any better than Pete?*

The idea of making him a goalie had stunned

Bill when the coach broached it before the game. It still left him shocked. He thought about it while he watched Northern increase the tempo of play. They were putting on the pressure, determined to break the tie score. Cliff Beardsley broke up the attack by stealing the puck in a clever maneuver.

Beardsley skated fast straight down the middle lane. It looked as though he was going to get off a shot. But the Northern center was a sharp player. He stole the puck from Beardsley.

Beardsley clamped his left elbow over his opponent's stick while he poked at the puck with his own club. The referee shrilled his whistle.

"Holding!" the official cried. He pointed at Beardsley, then at the penalty box.

Bill Jones fastened the strap of his head guard. He vaulted over the boards. He did not wait for a signal from Coach Le Beau. Beardsley would be in the penalty box for two minutes and Bill was Meinland's best penalty-time killer. A defense man skated to the box to make room for Bill on the ice. Beardsley was protesting to the referee.

"Knock it off!" Bill said shortly.

Beardsley glared.

"I thought a captain was supposed to stick up for his guys! We always did back East when a ref handed us a raw deal!"

14

"Don't be so cocky, you've got no beef." Bill eyed the blond newcomer. "It was holding all the way!"

Bill lost the puck at the faceoff. He darted around a Northern man. He hooked the skidding puck an instant before a Northern stick would have snaked it clear.

Bill stick-handled the rubber disk. He weaved back and forth in the neutral zone, killing time. Two Northern men converged to pin him against the boards. Bill slipped a pass to Walt Pickering, left wing of Meinland's second line. Walt drove across the blue line. There was no one between him and a breakaway shot at goal. He had only the goalie to beat.

Walt made a mistake in holding off his shot too long. Twenty feet out, as Walt tensed his wrists for a shot, the hard-skating Northern center hooked the puck off Walt's stick from behind. Walt whirled. He and the center crashed together and sprawled to the ice.

Bill took in the situation at a glance. If he charged for the puck and missed, Northern would have an opportunity for a power sweep with three-on-two. Bill skated fast diagonally across his own blue line.

He could not have timed things better.

A Northern wing dragged along the blue line

to keep from being offside. Bill intercepted the pass intended for the wing. He "ragged" the puck. Bill and Walt Pickering together killed the two minutes of Beardsley's penalty-box stay without allowing Northern a power rush on Pete Tinsley. Then Bill got a surprise.

Beardsley came out of the penalty box. Rusty Hanlon and Dick Carney came from the players' box. Beardsley started to skate off the ice. But Rusty motioned him back.

"Coach says you need a breather," Rusty said hurriedly to Bill. The replacements were being made with no stoppage of play. "Beardsley will center our line."

Bill stared incredulously. He looked toward the box. Coach was motioning him off. Bill skated to the box.

"You didn't get much rest before you were back out there," Coach Le Beau said. "Nice going, killing the penalty time. You earned a breather."

Bill looked at him steadily. The coach held his gaze. This just wasn't the way Coach operated. He kept his lines working intact as much as possible. Just what was going on?

Captain Bill Jones, center for Meinland's top production line, glued his gaze to Cliff Beardsley. There was no doubt about it. Beardsley was

16

good. He's a better skater than I am, Bill thought. And he sure can handle that stick.

Rusty snared the puck from an opponent. He passed to Dick. The wings whizzed the disk back and forth, bored in on the goal. A defense man checked Rusty. Rusty's pass to Beardsley was wobbly. But the blond newcomer snared the puck. He was 30 feet out and to the right of the cage. He charged in, faked a shot at the left corner. The goalie surged across the goal mouth. Beardsley blasted a hard backhand shot to the opposite corner.

The puck all but knocked the goalie's stick from his grasp. The rubber disk dribbled off the wood and fell over the goal line.

"Zowie!" Bill yelled. He rapped his stick against the boards in front of the players' box. "Stay hot out there, gang! Pour it on!"

The score was 5–4 now. Meinland was ahead for the first time in the game. Their lead lasted exactly eight seconds before Northern's production line produced the tying goal.

It came from a feint past Beardsley by the center, a sharp pass to a wing who slapped the puck by Pete Tinsley. Pete had again been caught badly out of position. But Beardsley should have blocked the center's pass.

Cliff Beardsley skated past the goal. He said something to Pete. Bill saw Pete shake his head. Pete's face was drawn and tense.

Northern scored their sixth goal thirty seconds later. Then with a 6–5 lead and the scoreboard clock blinking thirty-eight seconds of playing time left, Northern began killing time. The center stick-handled the puck cleverly in the neutral zone. Twenty seconds left. Ten. Five. The Northern center swerved around Beardsley's half-hearted check. He cut sharply and sped across the blue line. He banged the puck against the boards to avoid another sloppy check from Beardsley.

Pete Tinsley came out of the nets, trying to reach the puck as the disk skittered five feet outside the goal crease. It proved to be a foolish move. The center charged in. He rammed the puck into the open cage a second's fraction before the game-ending buzzer sounded.

Northern High, 7; Meinland High, 5.

Coach Le Beau stood in the players' box. His round face did not hold its usual placid expression.

"Five goals are a lot of counters," the coach said. "We have a potent attack. Five goals should be enough to win—but not when a leaky defense allows the other team seven!"

Coach Le Beau looked at Bill.

"You'd better give a lot of thought to the suggestion I made," the coach said. "We have a real goalkeeping problem."

That's not all, Bill thought. Getting Beardsley on the beam might not be easy, either!

CHAPTER 2

"You're on the Team, Too, Bill!"

Bill finished shoveling out the Jones' driveway Saturday morning. He stuck his head through the back doorway.

"Drive's cleared of snow, Mom," he called out loudly. "You can take the car out any time you—"

He broke off as his mother appeared from behind the opened door. She was wiping her hands on an apron.

"Hey, you'd better hurry!" Bill grinned. " 'Scuse me for yelling. I thought you were probably upstairs primping to go meet the plane Dad's boss is coming on."

"He isn't coming, dear. Your father phoned long distance just a few minutes ago. They've run into an unexpected problem on the job and all the —'top brass' was Will's expression—are flying up to meet him."

"Does that mean Dad won't be coming home when he's expected?"

"I'm afraid so, dear. He said that it probably would mean several weeks' delay."

Mrs. Jones eyed her son. Her eyes were a softer gray than Bill's, and her hair was not quite as dark. But anyone would have known they were mother and son.

"That's the way it happens sometimes with an engineer," she said. "We miss him a lot, don't we, Bill?"

"Of course. But we can carry things till he whips the job, I guess." Bill suddenly looked at his mother. He said, "Anything wrong with the way Bill, Jr., is handling the man-of-the-house stuff?"

"No, dear, no! But—" Again Mrs. Jones looked at her son closely. "Well, I've been wondering since breakfast what's bothering you. Will and you have always been so close. I'm fully aware that there are things—sometimes things come up that—oh, dear! I'm not making much sense, am I? What I'm trying to say is that if something is bothering you that could be helped by talking out, I'm a very good listener."

Bill frowned. So his problems showed that openly! For a moment he mentally debated whether to lay everything on the line to Mom. Mom was the greatest. But she'd never understand the way Dad would.

21

"Maybe all that's really bothering me is that I still have to chip the ice off the front steps," he said. He smiled. "And I want to go for a skate. If there's nothing else after the chipping job, guess I'll skip over to school and get my skates out of my gym locker."

He did not mention that the primary purpose of going to the school was to catch Le Beau if he happened to be in his office, as he usually was on Saturday mornings. Mrs. Jones nodded, gave a half sigh, then smiled.

"It's beyond me," she said. "Two hours of hockey practice every school day. And you skate every possible minute during weekends!"

"There's a thing I need to think out, Mom. Guess I think better skating."

A custodian let him into the school building. He told Bill that he had seen Mr. Le Beau in the hall outside his office not long before. The coach did not appear surprised when he answered Bill's rap on the door.

"I counted on your looking me up today," Le Beau said.

Bill gave the coach a quick look.

"Okay," Bill said. "There's no use stalling around, I guess. I just can't see this business of trying to make me into a goalie! You're coach. If you told me I *had* to play goalie—well, I'd try it.

22

But I wouldn't like it. I don't think we'd strengthen the team any! I don't think I'd make a good goalie!"

Le Beau just eyed Bill for a moment. When the coach spoke, his tone was mild.

"First of all," he said, "I'm not going to force you to try goalkeeping. There won't be any iron-glove stuff from me. However, I think a few things need to be made clear. This isn't something I just picked out of the blue. It has been in my mind since I learned that Hoad was moving from Meinland. I am convinced that you would make a fine goalkeeper. I'm convinced that the team would be much stronger with you in the nets."

"Why? I've never played goalie! I don't see—"

"Never?" the coach interrupted. He held Bill's gaze while a small smile played around the corners of his mouth. "You've never played goalie?"

Bill flushed a little.

"Oh, well," he said. "I fooled around with pads and stuff when I first began playing hockey. I meant I've never played goalie in a real game."

Bill gave the coach an odd look. He said curiously, "How'd you know I even fooled around with goalie stuff?"

"I've been coaching Meinland High hockey eleven years." The smile on Le Beau's face widened. "I doubt if any youngster in the community

23

plays around very long with a hockey stick before I know it. Part of a coach's job is to keep tab on material coming up. Quite some time before the boy gets to high school, Bill."

"Okay, so I did monkey around at goalkeeping." Bill shrugged. "I wasn't so hot at it. I didn't want to be a goalie. I still don't want to be a goalie. Doesn't a fellow have to *want* to do something if he's to do a good job at it? What's the matter with Pete Tinsley? Pete *wants* to be a goalie!"

"Desire is a major part in the make-up of an athlete." Coach Le Beau nodded. "Especially in hockey, football—any contact sport. But desire isn't everything. A boy must have capabilities—physical and mental and emotional capabilities. Tinsley lacks some very essential capabilities. I doubt that he would ever develop into a really good goalkeeper."

Bill looked puzzled. The coach must have noticed his confusion.

"You're pretty levelheaded," the coach said. "I'm going to be frank because I know you won't take it wrong and it will be strictly between us. Pete Tinsley happens to be too high-strung. He's oversensitive to criticism. Because he *wants* so much to be a goalkeeper, he's overanxious and easy for a clever opponent to fool.

"Tinsley's desire, no matter how strong, just can't overcome his natural handicaps. You don't have those handicaps. Don't get the idea that Tinsley is to be dropped from the squad. I believe that he can be developed into a first-class defense man."

Bill said slowly, "What about Rusty's and Dick's and my line? Suppose I tried goalkeeping and flopped?"

"I believe Beardsley would work in well with Rusty and Dick." The coach held Bill's gaze. "You just couldn't deliberately try to fail at goalkeeping. If it turned out that you—but I'm very sure that you'd be a better goalkeeper right now, with no experience, than Tinsley."

"You're a senior," the coach went on. "You're the best playmaker of all the centers in the Border Conference. I'm aware that there are many things to consider. That's why I tell you that there will be no pressure from me. There's no doubt in my mind that Meinland High will be a far stronger hockey team if you decide to give goalkeeping a try. But it has to be your decision."

Bill did not hesitate. He shook his head.

"I'm center on the Hanlon-Jones-Carney line," he said.

"It has to be your decision," the coach repeated.

Bill was quite uneasy as he left the school. He was not exactly pleased to find Peggy Sawyer outside.

"Hi," Peggy said. "I phoned to see if you were going skating and your mother told me you'd come over here.

"I hope you want company," she said.

She smiled and a dimple crinkled one cheek. She wore buff-colored ski pants and a matching windbreaker. A questioning expression came into her blue eyes as she looked at Bill. Bill hadn't realized that he had been scowling.

"But I guess you don't want company," Peggy said. "I didn't mean to—"

"Maybe company is what I need." Bill suddenly cut through her words.

Peggy was a good scout. She was a year younger than Bill. The Sawyers and the Joneses lived on the same block. Peggy had played baseball and football and hockey with Bill and other neighborhood boys until three or four years ago. Peggy's mother had more than once bewailed the fact that her daughter was more tomboy than girl.

"Maybe I need somebody's shoulder to cry on," Bill said. "How would you enjoy being a crying towel, Peg?"

"I'd make a good one." The dimple flashed.

"I hope you want company," she said

Bill told her that Le Beau was trying to persuade him to be a goalkeeper. He told her that he didn't want any part of it. He talked as if he was trying to convince himself, as well as her, that he was right and Coach was all wet.

"I remember you used to fool around with Terry's goalkeeping things," Peggy said, "the year that Aunt Bertha was in the hospital and Terry spent Christmas vacation at our house. You didn't seem so against goalkeeping then."

Bill gave her a quick look.

"I was ten years old," he said. "Any kid that age would be intrigued by goalie pads and the big stick. Quick as I found out how much better Terry was at it—well, I liked playing center a lot more. I still do!"

"There's more though, isn't there, Bill?"

"Okay!" Bill's tone was oddly defensive. "I want to stay at center because there's a good chance I'd get the Conference Hockey Award. You know that one senior of each conference school is given the Border Conference Hockey Award. It doesn't carry any guarantee that a fellow will make his college team, but it helps get attention from college hockey coaches.

"It's not an absolute must, of course, but I want to take my college work at Northern Tech. Dad took his degree from Northern. I'm not good enough in math and science to follow Dad's footsteps in engineering, but they have other courses besides engineering at Tech. The thing is, I want to play hockey in college."

Peggy looked puzzled. She said, "I must have missed something. I don't see what your wanting to go to Northern Tech has to do with keeping you from trying goalkeeping."

"Huh!" Bill snorted. "Terry Sawyer's your cousin. You ought to know he's the best goalie ever to come out of the Border Conference. He's better right now as goalie for the Frosh team than Tech's Varsity goalkeeper. It's a cinch that Tech won't be looking for goalkeepers for at least three years when Terry is eligible for the Varsity next year!"

Bill stopped speaking. He and Peggy walked almost across the bridge spanning Twin Forks River, and Peggy said nothing.

"Well?" Bill said. "Say something! Le Beau could be wrong. Pete will find himself. I know Rusty and Dick and I would have a good season. Maybe Beardsley would louse up a good line."

Peggy looked at him, then looked away.

"It's partly Cliff Beardsley, too, isn't it?" she asked.

Bill flushed. "Okay, so maybe it is," he admitted. "He's so darned cocky!"

29

"He's new, Bill. I don't know. Maybe he's just—just—well, you're the star player. You're the one Cliff Beardsley has to beat if he's going to be the star center. Maybe he isn't really like—like —oh, you know what I mean!"

"Sure. You think I'm being selfish! Why don't you come right out and say it!"

"Mr. Le Beau got to philosophizing in social-problems class the other day," Peggy said slowly. "According to him, everybody is selfish. Some of us a little more than others. I think I see your position."

"But you also think I should listen to Le Beau!"

"I didn't say that. It seems to me that it comes down to how much you think of the team, Bill."

"How much I think of the team? For crying all over the ice! I'm captain!"

Peggy looked up. Her blue eyes were troubled.

"I don't really know how a boy thinks, of course," she said. "They elected you captain. It's quite an honor. Also it's quite a responsibility. You're captain—but you're on the team, too, Bill!"

CHAPTER 3

Opening Game

Morall High would come to Meinland High's rink to open the Conference schedule Thursday afternoon. It was the only game scheduled for Meinland until after Christmas vacation.

Bill just could not help it. He told himself that it was because of things Le Beau had planted in his mind. He kept noticing mistakes that Pete Tinsley made as the team practiced for the Morall game.

Pete allowed nine goals in a thirty-minute scrimmage during Monday practice. The goals were equally divided among the three front lines that Le Beau used. So Pete's bad afternoon could not be attributed to any special fine play used by one particular attacking line. Pete was dejected as the boys skated from the ice.

"Everybody was hotter than little red wagons," Rusty Hanlon said. "We sure shot a flurry of pucks at you, Pete!"

The long face of Pete Tinsley became longer. He looked down at Rusty.

31

"It was more than a flurry," Pete said. "It was a blizzard!"

Bill eyed the tall goalie curiously. He liked Pete. Bill was amazed and a little aghast at the words he spoke.

"You don't keep your eye on the puck!" Bill said. "You get too anxious and go for a save before the guy shooting gets off his shot! You let the shooters fake you out of position!"

Pete winced almost as though Bill had slapped him.

"Beardsley told me the same thing the other day," he said. He added miserably, "Looks like I can't do anything right!"

"Oh, come off it!" Rusty chunked the taller boy in the ribs. "So you had a rough half-hour today. Probably tomorrow you'll give us a rougher time than we gave you today. Everybody has a bad day once in a while, Pete!"

"Yeah, I guess so." Pete's tone was bleak. "But a fellow ought to have a good day once in a while —if he's any good!"

Pete skated to a bench outside the rink and began removing his goalie pads. Rusty eyed Bill.

"Weren't you pretty rough on him?" Rusty asked. "The poor guy needs his confidence built up, not criticism!"

"I know it!" Bill spoke shortly. He wished he had kept his mouth shut. "I shouldn't have said anything. It's the truth, though, and I—oh, nuts!"

Bill's mind went back to the things Coach Le Beau had said. Oversensitive. Nervous. Over-anxious. All the things that Le Beau had mentioned certainly fitted Pete.

Pete Tinsley was not much better in the nets on Tuesday. Coach Le Beau stressed a thing in that practice that Bill had been wondering about. Most of that session was devoted to defensive tactics.

"The greatest goalkeeper who ever played hockey couldn't stop every shot," Le Beau said. "The man with the puck has the advantage. He knows where he is going and what maneuver he is going to try. He can wait till the goalkeeper commits himself. Give the attacker time and he has all the edge on the goal tender. It's up to the defense to see that the attacker doesn't have that time."

The coach alternated front lines and defense men. He seemed to have eyes on both sides and in the back of his head.

"You're loafing, Rusty! Back-checking is part of hockey, you know! . . . You let him have all day to pass, Buck! Harass him! . . . You've got to get so you can skate backwards. Slow him down! Slow him down! There are such things as body checks, you know! . . . No, no, no! Beardsley, hockey is a two-way street. The instant your team loses possession of the puck, you're on defense! D-E-F-E-N-S-E! Get back and make it tough for the attack to maneuver in the scoring area!"

Pete Tinsley did not allow nine goals that practice. But no matter how stiff a defense his defense men and forwards put up, in the final analysis the goalie has to make the saves. No defense can throttle an attack so thoroughly that there are no opportunities for shots.

Two of the five goals that were scored against Pete would have been cleared by a sharp goalie.

Coach Le Beau devoted most of the Wednesday practice to smoothing out passing and play patterns. The Hanlon-Jones-Carney line and the Dalton-Beardsley-Pickering line worked the puck into scoring area time and again.

"Nobody can tell me we aren't going to blink that old red light plenty!" Rusty Hanlon enthused. "If we don't crash a dozen or more past the Morall goalie, I'll eat my hockey stick!"

"Morall is doped to be weak again this year," Dick Carney said. "We should take 'em. But a dozen goals would be a lot of goals—and a hockey stick would be kind of hard to digest!"

"I'll be happy if Morall doesn't get a dozen against us!" Bill said.

"Oh, come off it!" Rusty gave Bill an odd look. "Morall didn't have much last year in the way of offense. And they lost all of their best front line and two of their second line by graduation. Pete will probably hold Morall to a goal or two. Maybe he'll hang a horse collar on them. A shutout would be a thing to boost his confidence, I guess!"

"A shutout would be something to put in a believe-it-or-not column!"

Bill spoke morosely. Again Rusty looked puzzled.

"What the heck's eating you?" Rusty said. "You've been off the beam since we scrimmaged Northern. It's not like you to take such a dim view of things, Bill!"

Bill opened his mouth to snap back at Rusty. He closed it abruptly. None of the fellows knew that Le Beau was trying to sell him on playing goalie. Okay, you told Le Beau it was no sale. Stop thinking about it. Concentrate on playing center. It's up to Le Beau to develop a goalie!

But it was easier to tell yourself to stop thinking than to stop. As the referee stood outside the center circle for the opening faceoff of the Morall game, Bill found himself worrying about Pete Tinsley in the nets.

If Morall High—the weakest team in the Border Conference—scored easily against Pete, the goalie situation would be rougher than ever.

Bill whacked the puck to Rusty on the faceoff. Rusty broke toward the right boards. Morall's defense back-pedaled. Bill swung to center ice. Dick Carney trailed Bill. It was a play they had practiced many times.

"Set, Rusty!" Bill yelled. "Here we go!"

Bill took Rusty's pass 15 feet from the blue line. Rusty cut fast diagonally toward the goal cage. Bill bit his skates into ice as though he was going to try a straight-on drive at the goal. Two Morall boys skated to cut him off. Bill stopped dead. He flipped a pass back and Dick was there. Dick did not hold the puck. He flicked the disk and Rusty picked it up and had only the goalie to beat.

Rusty feinted nicely. He forced the goalie to commit himself. Rusty lofted the puck over the goalie's outflung body. The red light flared.

"Beautiful!" Rusty yelled. He whacked Bill on the shoulder. "A perfect play. You set 'em up like that and we'll get *two* dozen light-blinkers!"

The Hanlon-Jones-Carney line scored again less than forty seconds later. Pete Tinsley turned back the first Morall sortie into Meinland ice. He cleared the puck to Bob Moore. Bob swept around back of the nets with such speed that he found a lane clear down the left boards. Bob carried the puck solo well into Morall ice.

An instant before he was checked, Bob flipped the puck to Dick Carney. Dick blasted a hard shot

that the Morall goalie managed to get in front of. But the puck rebounded from his pads. Before he could clear, Bill roared across outside the crease and poked the disk over the goal line.

Meinland, 2; Morall, 0.

Coach Le Beau changed lines and defense men. "Didn't I tell you!" Rusty yelled exuberantly as they skated to the players' box. "Pete smothered that one and we beat their goalie two out of three times. Who can hang crepe when we go like that, Bill?"

Captain Bill Jones said nothing. He watched the Dalton-Beardsley-Pickering line. Cliff Beardsley sure could skate. And he was a clever stickhandler.

Bill suddenly frowned. Maybe he was not seeing things in proper proportion. Maybe he was edgy toward Beardsley. But he knew deep down that Beardsley had muffed a fine chance for a pass to Walt. Instead, a Morall wing had snaked the puck away from Beardsley.

The Morall attack formed and swept across the blue line. Bill cried to himself, "Back-check! Back-check!" But Cliff Beardsley did not back-check. Morall had a three-on-two setup. Hank Brown, left defense, had to commit himself. He went after the wing. The Morall boy waited just the right length of time. He passed an instant before Hank's check. The puck was centered perfectly—too far outside the crease unless Pete left his cage.

Pete Tinsley did not leave his cage. He was fooled. He scrambled across the goal cage mouth.

He committed himself too soon. A Morall wing scooted in and beat Pete with a hard, angled shot to the side of the cage that Pete had left.

Bill groaned. He said, "Overanxious again! Why didn't he come out and smother the puck!" He did not realize that he spoke aloud.

Rusty looked queerly at the team captain. Rusty said, "My gosh! Any goalie goofs once in a while! Give Pete a chance, Bill!"

There was little doubt of the eventual outcome of the game after Cliff Beardsley cashed a third Meinland goal ten seconds before Le Beau changed lines. Meinland's third front line scored another goal. But in the two minutes they were on the ice, Morall High beat Pete Tinsley again. It was 4–2 as the buzzer sounded ending the first period.

Bill Jones scored his second goal midway of the second period. Cliff Beardsley cashed a brilliant solo effort, stick-handled his way almost to the crease, then deked the goalie with a clever backhand-to-forehand shift from 6 feet out.

Bill Jones and Cliff Beardsley both achieved the coveted "hat trick"—scoring three goals in one game—during the third period. Bill's did not come until he slammed a rebound past the goal-keeper eight seconds before the game-ending buzzer.

Meinland High, 12; Morall High, 7.

That was the score on the board at the finish. Rusty Hanlon heaved a mock sigh.

"I was sure glad to see you cash that last light-blinker," he said to Bill. "I was beginning to wonder just how a hockey stick would taste! But I guess we showed any Northern scouts present a thing or two!"

Bill was suddenly irritated.

"What is there to cheer about!" Bill's tone was sharper than he had intended. "Or didn't you notice that Morall scored seven goals? *Seven!*"

"You needn't bite a guy's head off!" Again Rusty's expression was puzzled. "We scored twelve. What's the diff if the other guys did—"

"Oh, nuts!" Bill interrupted. "Knock it off! When Morall can score seven goals, I hate to think how many Falls City and East Fork and West Fork will score. Not to mention Northern High!"

CHAPTER 4

Reluctant Decision

Christmas vacation would begin at noon Friday.
Meinland High students had no classes to prepare
that morning, and Bill Jones was restless during
his third-hour study period. He knew in his heart
that he would have been restless even if there had
been classes to prepare.

"Okay!" Bill muttered half aloud. "I might
as well get this thing off my chest!"

The study-hall teacher gave him a permission
slip to go to Mr. Le Beau's room. Le Beau had no
third-hour class. He looked up from his desk as
Bill came in. Le Beau said nothing. Bill frowned
a little as he looked at the coach.

"Okay!" Bill said. "You win. I'm willing to
give this goalkeeping thing a try. That's if Pete
Tinsley understands that I'm not trying to under-
mine him!"

Le Beau nodded. The expression on his round
face remained placid.

"Evidently you haven't seen Tinsley this morning," he said. "He came to me yesterday after the
game. It was his own idea. I had said nothing to

41

him. He feels that the team will be better off with someone else tending goal. He was pretty low. I think Tinsley is really relieved at the prospect of trying defense instead of goalkeeping. He turned in his pads, skates, and stick."

"You can probably turn them back to Pete after I flop as a goalie!" Bill scowled. "I'm not sold on all the talk you gave me about being a whiz at the job. But I'll practice as hard as I can during vacation. I'll give the thing all I have."

"That's all a coach can ask." Le Beau nodded. He seemed to be occupied with thoughts of things other than hockey for a moment. He said, "Mrs. Le Beau wrote her folks that we would spend Christmas with them. But I can talk her into waiting until the day before Christmas to leave. That will give us four days to work. Can you be at the rink this afternoon?"

Bill drew in a breath. He was irritated that Le Beau accepted everything so matter-of-factly. Just as though he'd counted on it all the time.

"I'll be there," Bill said shortly.

The coach was on skates when Bill arrived at the rink. Le Beau pointed to a pair of skates, a pair of goalie pads, a pair of goalie gloves, and a goalkeeper's stick on a bench. The stick had a blade 3½ inches wide instead of the standard 3-inch blade. The shaft was as wide as the blade for a distance of 24 inches from the heel. Bill eyed the skates.

"If the skates don't fit," Le Beau said, "I'll leave word at the Sports Shop to order new ones for you. A goalkeeper needs the old-type automobile skate to stand heavy knocks, and without space to allow the puck to get between skate and shoe. Try on the equipment."

Bill laced the skate shoes. They felt funny and awkward when he stood. But they fitted well. They seemed awkward because the blades were duller than those he was used to, and had more contact with the ice. That was a thing he would have to accept. A goalkeeper needs duller skates to slide from side to side more smoothly than he can with sharp skates, which bite into the ice.

The goalie pads made him feel as though he were skating with boards between his legs. The wide stick and the big gloves were cumbersome.

"Stance is pretty important in goalkeeping," Le Beau said. "We may as well start with stance. Your feet should be comfortably apart, toes slanted a little outward, heels closer together. Your body should be slightly bent from the waist. Your head is forward, but not to the point of strain or discomfort. Rest your stick with the blade in front of the feet and hold the stick loosely. Your free arm hangs loosely at your side. The palm should be turned toward the man coming at you with the puck. Try to keep your whole body as loose as possible. A goalkeeper should stay relaxed until the instant of decision. Try it."

Bill attempted to put into practice all that the coach had said. He felt awkward. He scowled. Le Beau smiled.

"I gave you too much at once," he said. "Just take a stance that feels easy to you."

Bill did so. He was surprised to see Le Beau nod in satisfaction.

"You're a natural," the coach said. "You're doing only one thing that could be criticized—you're gripping your stick too hard. I'll try a few shots and you stop them."

Le Beau did not make the shots too easy or soft, but they were straight-on shots. Bill turned them away easily, mostly by using his wide-blade stick.

"You're getting the feel," Le Beau said after a while. "I'm going to make them tougher."

The puck came off Le Beau's stick faster and from an angle. Bill managed to get his pads in front of the puck. He felt the shock as the hard rubber disk rebounded. He blocked six consecutive shots with his pads, or kicked them out with his skates, or knocked them aside with his stick. A comfortable feeling came to him. Why, it could be this goalkeeping thing wasn't so tough!

Le Beau swooped in on the cage from the right. Bill closed his pads and crouched in front of that corner. Le Beau swept past and for just an instant Bill unconsciously relaxed. The puck whistled off Le Beau's stick. It was a backhand shot aimed at the opposite corner and two feet off the ice. Bill jabbed his stick. He did not touch the puck. The disk bellied the net. The comfortable feeling drained from Bill.

"Swell shot," he said. He fished the puck from beneath the cords with his stick. "You fooled me good."

"It was a good shot," Le Beau admitted. He smiled. "I wouldn't have bet I could have controlled it." He skated away with the puck, then said over his shoulder, "That kind just about has to be a glove save, Bill."

Bill was angry—at himself. Anybody who ever saw a hockey shot should have known that! "Try it again," he said grimly.

This time Le Beau did not carry the puck across the front of the goal crease. He blazed a shot at about the same height. Bill lunged his free hand but he did not make a glove save. The puck was wide of the goal mouth.

"I didn't think I could do it right along." Le Beau sighed. "You'd have stopped that one if I'd got it in there."

"You had me beat." Bill grunted. "Try some more of those, huh?"

Le Beau swept in. It crossed Bill's mind that the coach must have been a star in his active playing days. Bill could not remember ever having seen a harder shot. He felt great satisfaction when

he caught two of the five hard shots that Le Beau blistered at the cage.

"We'll call it a day," Le Beau said after nearly an hour. A grin wrinkled his round face. "I'm bushed! You're going to be a very tough goalkeeper to beat, Bill!"

"Yeah!" Bill scowled. "I missed four out of six when you really banged 'em!"

46

"You can't expect to absorb everything in one practice. You'll come along. You're a natural." The coach skated to his jacket on a bench. He took folded papers from a pocket. He handed them to Bill.

"I got together a few things that might give you some help," the coach said. "Just a few. Books have been written on goalkeeping technique without covering everything. See you tomorrow?"

Bill nodded. He glanced at the typed sheets, noted a few headings. Positional Play. Playing a Shooter. Playing a Deker. Smothering the Puck. Using the Hands. Using the Stick. Using the Body. Clearing the Puck.

Just a few!

He read and reread the goalkeeping tips that night.

GOALKEEPING TIPS
FOR BILL JONES

Positional Play: A position well out in front, near the end of the goal crease, lessens the angle of any shot. The goalkeeper is thus able to retreat a little if necessary to keep in line with the puck.

Playing a Shooter: Best to keep the body directly in line with angle of the shooter's stick blade. Close in on the puck as soon as possible when the puck carrier is known to be a shooter. Practically all hockey players follow a pattern. The goalkeeper must keep a "book" on opponents. Do not try to guess, but you can anticipate the

47

likely move when you know the opponent's pattern.

Playing a Deker: The attacker who favors bringing the puck far in and attempting to beat the goalie with a stick-handling trick—a deker—must be played alertly. Watch your stance. Keep your body in line with the puck. Move to the edge of your crease or even in front of it so that you will have time to back up a bit as the deker comes in. Try to force the opponent into a first move.

Smothering the Puck: Drop on the puck and smother it any time there is an opponent close to the puck and you can beat him to it. Do not dive or belly-flop on the puck to smother. Drop to the knees and grab it and curl the body around it. You cannot dive forward as fast as you can skate. If the puck is some distance out, skate a stride or two and then smother. It is a good idea to drop your stick to leave both hands free in smothering the puck.

Using the Hands: You can cover the most space in the shortest time by using your hands. Your hands are your best weapons. Hand saves give better control of the puck rebound. Arms and shoulders kept loose and relaxed allow the hands to move with greatest accuracy and speed.

Using the Stick: The stick is used to clear the puck, to stick-check or intercept passes, to block shots. Hold the stick loosely. A tight grip develops tension and fatigue. A loosely held stick absorbs the force of a blocked shot and allows much less rebound. Learn to shift the stick from hand to hand.

Using the Body: A hard shot can break through a skate, stick, or hand, but it cannot move a body. Get your body in front of every shot you possibly can. Ideally, use the body to block the shot, then the hand to trap the puck. Thus you control the rebound. Keep the body square toward the puck. The squarer the body toward the puck, the larger the goal area it covers.

Clearing the Puck: Goals are scored from rebounds. When there is danger of a rebound being poked in by an opponent, smother the puck. The puck should always be cleared to the side and behind the goal when possible. Clear by passing to a teammate only when you are sure the pass cannot be intercepted. Clear as soon as possible to lessen opportunity for an opponent to break for the puck.

Bill was at the rink early Saturday morning. Pete Tinsley came a few minutes after Bill arrived.

"I saw you and Coach working out yesterday," Pete said. He eyed the goalie equipment that Bill wore, and a wistful expression shadowed his longish face for a moment. "It looked to me as if you were better just starting out than I ever will be," Pete said. "What I was wondering is whether I could sort of practice with you? I probably couldn't give you any help, but it's a cinch you could give me tips on stuff a fellow needs to play defense."

"There's plenty I don't know about goalkeep-

49

ing," Bill said. "Could be we can help each other."

Coach Le Beau came. Pete Tinsley asked him if it was all right.

"Good enough." Le Beau nodded. "A defense man has to be as much a forward when he gets the puck in the scoring area as a forward has to be defense man when the other team is attacking. The more different styles of shooting Bill has to practice against, the better."

Le Beau gave Bill intensive coaching during the workout.

"You can fake the shooter as well as letting him fake you. Faking a stick-check often fools the puck carrier into committing himself. . . . A goalkeeper must think of every shot as a tough one. What should be easy saves and long shots often score when a goalkeeper gets careless. . . . You leave the net only when you're absolutely sure you can get to the puck first. . . . Keep cool. Wait for the puck carrier to make his move. A goalkeeper who moves too soon is a goalkeeper easy to beat. . . ."

They did not practice Sunday. Monday brought Rusty Hanlon and Cliff Beardsley and Dick Carney to the rink. Hank Brown dropped by with Pete Tinsley. It was almost like a regular team practice. Bill Jones got plenty of practice in the nets. He had to force his attention away from the

50

Hanlon-Beardsley-Carney front line to concentrate on the coaching Le Beau gave him.

Bill was irritable following practice the morning of the day before Christmas.

"I'm a chump," he told Rusty Hanlon. "This goalie thing is for the birds. I'm wasting my time!"

"Hunh-uh." Rusty shook his head. "You're wrong, Bill. We're going to be a lot better off with you tending that old cage. You're going to be—"

"Yeah, yeah, yeah!" Bill interrupted. "Better than Ben was! Better than Terry Sawyer, I suppose! Knock it off. Le Beau's handed me that song and dance until I'm sick of it! I wish I'd never told him I'd do it!"

But despite his flare-up at Rusty, Bill found himself looking forward to daily workouts in the goal cage. Terry Sawyer came with his parents to visit Peggy Sawyer's folks New Year's Day. The former star Northern High goalie naturally gravitated to Meinland's hockey rink. He grinned at Bill.

"Peg gave me the dope," Terry said. "Mind if I horn in on this a little?"

Terry's enjoyment at skating without goalie pads, taking shots at Bill, and playing wing in a scrimmage that developed was evident. Bill felt a glow when Terry complimented him as the session broke up.

"You handle that big stick and stuff as though you'd always played goalie," Terry said. "Maybe a few little tricks you need to pick up. If I can help you, let me know."

Bill looked at the Northern Tech freshman star quickly.

"I hope you aren't just saying that," Bill said. "I'd sure appreciate tips from a *good* goalie!"

"I mean it." Terry grinned. "Fact is, I might learn something from you, too!"

Bill felt fine. Then Terry suddenly asked a question.

"Where are you headed for, Bill? I mean, where are you going to college?"

Bill abruptly did not feel so fine. All the dormant resentment welled up in him.

"I've always thought I'd go to Tech," he said slowly. "I want to play college hockey. But it's a sure thing that Tech coaches won't be interested in a green-as-a-gourd goalie with you coming up!"

"Hockey coaches are always interested in goalies." Terry grinned. "Personally, I'd just as soon you didn't come to Tech. You'll be tough competition with a season or two of experience."

"Nuts!"

Terry's grin widened. He said, "What's to keep you from going out for center again when you come to Tech?"

"After wasting a year learning new techniques and forgetting all I knew about playing center? I'd be half goalie and half center—and no good at either one!"

"You have a point, I guess." Terry nodded. "But there are other top schools that play hockey. You might get a better deal from another school than from Tech. Suppose you do have a lot to learn about goalkeeping. What goalie doesn't have things to learn? But I'd say you've got what it takes. And that's not kidding, Bill. Stick with it."

"Thanks—" Bill said, "for nothing! As far as I'm concerned, goalkeeping is for the birds—but I'm stuck with it!"

CHAPTER 5

A Goalie Has a Cinch

Bill gave himself pep talks all during the remainder of the vacation. He knew that he had not adjusted well to changing from center on Meinland's first line to goalie. But he did his best to accept the shift and assured himself that he had smothered his resentment.

Then Cliff Beardsley began popping off at the first practice after vacation.

The first shot that Beardsley tried in the warmup was a straight-on blast. Bill easily, almost lazily, turned the puck aside with his stick.

"Well, well, well!" Beardsley widened his eyes. "What have we here? A Vezina Trophy puck grabber, no less!"

It could have been a compliment. The Vezina Trophy is awarded each year to the goalie in the National Hockey League who has the least goals scored against him in League play. It could have been a compliment—but not the way Beardsley said it. The "puck grabber" ground on Bill. He eyed the blond newcomer.

"Doesn't take much of a puck grabber to stop soft ones," Bill said.

Beardsley gave him a quick look. "Like that, huh!" Beardsley grunted. "Try the next one for size, puck grabber!"

A few minutes later the puck came to Beardsley. He skated back across the blue line and came thundering in. He could skate. He could handle the puck. Bill crouched in front of the cage. He watched Beardsley closely. Instinct warned him when Beardsley shoulder-feinted right. Bill did not fall for the fake.

He lined his body directly in the path of Beardsley's shot. He was ready for the ankle-high sizzler that Beardsley powered toward the cage. The puck thudded against his pads. Bill trapped the rebound with his stick and slid the disk aside.

"A little better," Bill said as Beardsley flashed across in front of the crease. "I could almost feel that one!"

Beardsley scowled. Bill was quite aware that from then on the slender blond put everything he had in every shot. He was also aware that the satisfaction that he felt was not warranted by the mere turning aside of practice shots.

The satisfaction that filled him after thirty minutes of scrimmage was different. He had turned back the best efforts of three attacking lines that

Coach Le Beau used, until Rusty Hanlon beat him just before Coach whistled an end to practice.

Rusty's goal came on a poke of a rebound from a tough save Bill made on a half-screened shot from Dick Carney.

Bill sprawled across the crease and lunged out a gloved hand to smother the rebound. Rusty's stick was a fraction of a second quicker. The glove was knocked from Bill's hand as the disk skittered across the goal line. Rusty was quickly concerned.

"Gosh, are you hurt, Bill? I didn't mean to whack your hand. I—"

"It's okay." Bill rubbed his reddened knuckles. "But I'm sure glad goalies wear extra padded gloves!"

"Man, I'm telling you!" Sincere admiration was in Rusty's tone as he jabbed Bill in the ribs. "You're a goalie—and I mean *goalie!* I don't see how you got in front of Dick's shot. And you came doggone close to getting mine!"

"Close only counts in pitching horseshoes," Bill said. "I should have trapped the rebound."

"Listen to the guy!" Dick Carney scoffed. "He robs me of a goal with a nearly impossible save and then gripes about missing an absolutely impossible one!"

"You sure did a job," Pete Tinsley said. Pete's

tone held a wistfulness. "If I could handle a goalie stick and pads like you did—well, I couldn't and that's that!"

"What's all the cheering about?" Cliff Beardsley said sarcastically. "They give a goalie pads that practically cover the cage mouth and gloves that cover what the pads don't. All he has to do is stand there and block a little space six feet wide and four feet high. A goalie has a cinch!"

Coach Le Beau skated from behind Bill at that moment. Whatever Bill might have retorted was never said.

"You looked great, Bill," the coach said. "Goal tending like that will pay off big for us."

Bill did not stop every shot aimed his way during that week of practice. Each day Coach Le Beau pointed out a few things. But after the final practice before Meinland was to go to West Fork High for the second Conference game, Le Beau praised Bill highly.

"You react just as I was sure you would," Le Beau said. "They don't fool you a second time with the same maneuver. You haven't made the same mistake twice. That's the mark of a good goalkeeper. We're a much better team with you tending goal. You've sharpened our attack, too."

"Sharpened our attack?" Bill looked as puzzled as his tone indicated. "I appreciate the kind words, Coach. But it's pretty hard to believe that a goalie sharpens a team's attack."

"It's a hockey axiom that every coach recognizes," Le Beau said. "You have a man in the nets who is tough to beat and your forwards develop skating and shooting skills trying to beat him in practice sessions. Those skills carry over and your attack is much sharper in games."

The West Fork game certainly seemed to bear out Coach Le Beau's contention. The Hanlon-Beardsley-Carney line beat the West Fork goalie in the first minute of play. The goal came off a nicely executed play pattern.

Beardsley snared a loose puck in the neutral zone. He skated across the blue line fast. He barreled straight down the center lane. A West Fork defense man dashed across to cover and left Rusty Hanlon free ten feet out from the right boards. Beardsley smartly fooled the defense, passed to Dick Carney. Dick swept the puck diagonally across and Rusty was there. Rusty drove in on the goal, drew the goalie across to protect the near corner.

Rusty blazed a hard shot. The puck was perhaps ten inches off the ice. It caught the left lobe of the netting even as the goalie belatedly jabbed a glove.

Meinland kept pressure on West Fork. Bill

made only four saves during the first period. At 14:38 of the period—twenty-two seconds before the end, since Border Conference games were played in fifteen-minute periods—Buck Dalton recovered a wild West Fork pass. Buck drove hard for the goal in a solo dash. The goalkeeper blocked Buck's shot. But Walt Pickering—centering the second line after Beardsley was moved up to take over Bill's first line position—pounced on the rebound. He beat the goalie with a sizzling forehand shot. The scoreboard showed nice figures as players skated off for intermission.

Meinland High, 2; West Fork High, 0.

"Nothing to it!" Rusty exulted as he skated off beside Bill. "You'll hang the old horse collar on 'em! And we're a breeze to blink that red light four or five times more!"

"They had tough luck on a lot of passes," Bill said. "If they settle down, we won't have the puck so much. A couple of their guys have real hard shots, too."

West Fork's rink was an outdoor rink. During the second period, the sky darkened and the wind freshened. Cliff Beardsley banged a beautiful shot into the netting after faking the goalie out of position midway of the period. The Schmidt-Elberry-Murray line, a trio of tenth-graders that Le Beau worked together for Meinland's third

59

line, scored their first goal of the season in the thirteenth minute of the second period. And flecks of snow began to drift with the wind across the rink at the faceoff following the goal. It was Meinland, 4; West Fork, 0, at the end of the period.

"Didn't I tell you this would be a breeze?" Rusty slapped Bill on the back in the dressing room. "You've got those Fork jokers measured right down to a T for the old horse collar!"

"That wind comes up harder and keeps carrying snow, it might turn into a blizzard instead of a breeze," Pete Tinsley said. He drew his brows together. "Blizzard. Now where did I hear that before? Oh, sure! But they haven't been throwing a blizzard of pucks at you, Bill."

"You guys have been sharp on defense." Bill nodded. "Four saves the first period and only seven the second. It sure hasn't been a blizzard yet!"

"Why couldn't it have happened to me?" Pete grinned. "But I'm not griping. It was a real thrill to get an assist on Murray's goal instead of being on the receiving end!"

The third period began in a snowstorm that allowed but poor vision. The storm gave every indication of developing into a full-scale blizzard as play went on.

"You stop any shots these jokers get in this thick

stuff, you're a wizard," Rusty said to Bill. "I don't even know where the puck is most of the time!"

It became increasingly difficult to follow the black disk as the final fifteen minutes of play dragged on. Passes went wild. Players skated frantically trying to locate the puck. Snow accumulating on the ice did not help skating. It seemed to Bill that they played an hour before somebody yelled, "Five minutes left!"

Neither goalie had been called on to make a save.

Bill squirmed back and forth across his crease. What chance would a fellow have to clear a shot in this stuff when he couldn't see a thing?

The wind shifted. Snow pelted Bill in the face. He could make out moving forms through the blizzard. But nobody could have told whether they were teammates or West Fork boys.

He could not see the scoreboard clock. Someone yelled, "Going into the last minute!"

Figures loomed dimly before Bill's vision. Two of them. He thought he could make out that one wore a jersey with the lower half dark. That would be a Meinland jersey, crimson below the white shoulders. Or was it a green West Fork jersey with snow covering the upper part?

Bill crouched in front of his goal cage. He

61

strained his eyes. Strain as he did, he could not make out clearly what was what. He thought that one of the figures had a black something cradled in the crook of his stick. The puck. But was it a teammate or a West Fork boy?

He wouldn't be barging in on you if he were a teammate!

Bill swiped a hand across his eyes. He could not wipe away the driving blizzard. But he caught a blur of motion through the storm. He flung his body full length to the ice and stretched his stick and gloved hands across the crease.

Thunk!

Something hard stung his chest. He loosed his grip on the stick and grabbed blindly with both gloves. He clutched the gloves to his body.

Smash!

Bill was suddenly tangled with a body, sprawled on top of him across the goal crease. Quick gasps of breath beat against Bill's ears. His head was pushed against the ice as the figure on top arose. A whistle shrilled.

"You lucky stiff!" It was a boy in the green of West Fork who made the cry. "How the heck did you see that puck!"

"You know something?" Bill grinned. "I didn't see it. I didn't know I had it. It was pure luck that—"

The grin abruptly washed from Bill's face. He stared at empty gloves. He had been sure that he trapped the puck between gloves and body after it hit his chest. But his gloves held no puck. Bill

scrambled erect, probed beneath his pads. The puck had to be there.

"Goal!" the referee suddenly shouted. He signaled the goal judge, and the red light flared. "Good goal," the referee said.

He pointed to the ice. The puck lay in such a

position that there might have been some room for argument about whether or not it was a goal. But Bill knew that the referee's decision was a fair one.

Bill hooked the puck with his stick, slithered it viciously toward the boards. Instantly he was sorry. He looked quickly at the referee.

"I'm not beefing," Bill said. "It was a goal— whether I carried the puck over the line or not. I'm not protesting!"

"Okay." The referee nodded. "I guess any goalie would be burned, losing a shutout in the last few seconds!"

There was a faceoff in the center circle following the West Fork goal. Almost immediately after the referee dropped the puck, the game-ending buzzer sounded.

Teammates surrounded Bill. They poured words of praise at him.

"Man, you're a *goalie!* You had them shut out till that freak goal! . . . Yeah, if it was a goal! I bet that West Fork guy batted it over with his glove! . . . Wow, did you ever play a game in those nets, Bill! . . . How about picking off a puck in a blinding blizzard? . . . They might as well give us that old Border Conference championship right now!"

There was but one discordant note.

64

Cliff Beardsley skated near Bill.

"What's so hot about holding a team to one goal? Don't they give a goalie all the breaks?   Just that one little patch of ice to stand around in—and a blizzard to keep the shooters from telling where the goal is!   A goalie has a cinch!"

CHAPTER 6

A Game Is Postponed

Bill lacked any great enthusiasm for table tennis. He played occasionally on the table in the Sawyers' basement. His lack of enthusiasm for the game could have stemmed from the fact that Peggy Sawyer beat him consistently. Then Coach Le Beau gave Bill a book on goalkeeping, and Bill's outlook toward table tennis changed.

> ... A goalkeeper will profit by playing games such as table tennis, badminton, handball and others in which the object in contention moves rapidly as does a hockey puck. Paying special attention to keeping his eyes on the rapidly moving object will tend to develop a habit pattern that will carry over to keeping his eyes on the puck when tending goal. ...

Bill read that paragraph in the book and formed a new outlook on table tennis. He began playing regularly with Peggy, evenings after schoolwork was done. He told himself that he would disregard winning or losing. He would concentrate on keeping his eye on the ball. Never mind who scored the points. He would play the goofy game only to develop a habit pattern.

"You're holding back!" Peggy accused the third evening they played. She had just beaten Bill by 21–19. "You could have won that last point and deuced the game!"

"I was lucky to come close," Bill said lazily.

"It's no fun if you let me win!"

"I haven't been letting you win," Bill said. "Maybe I haven't been bearing down all the time. I told you I only wanted to play because it might help my goalkeeping. Coach gave me a book that —well, never mind. Tell you what—from now on you give it everything you've got and I'll do the same."

"I always play as hard as I know how!"

They played four more games. Bill won three of them.

As hockey practice sessions went on, Bill found that he rarely lost sight of the puck. He enjoyed the daily battle between himself and the shooters. Coach Le Beau was frank in his satisfaction with Bill's play.

"I was sure you'd make a good goalkeeper," Le Beau said, "but you're developing faster than I figured. You're a natural in the cage. There's just one thing, Bill. No goalie can stop every shot. You're inclined to be bothered too much when a puck gets by you. Loss of equanimity, allowing himself to be too much concerned over the goal

67

just made against him, doesn't do a goalie any good. Wipe it from your mind and concentrate on turning back the next shot!"

Bill knew that Le Beau's advice was sound. He did a good job in following it—except when it was Cliff Beardsley who beat him. The battle between the slender center and Captain Bill Jones increased in tempo with every practice.

It was the day before Fall City High was scheduled to come to Meinland's rink that the feeling between Beardsley and Bill flared high.

Beardsley snared a loose puck in the neutral zone. Rusty Hanlon and Pete Tinsley were between Beardsley and the goal as Beardsley charged across the blue line. Either Rusty or Pete would have been in better position for a shot. But Beardsley did not pass. Rusty and Pete formed a screen for the center as Beardsley drove in. Beardsley shot. Bill lunged across the goal mouth. He darted out a hand and caught the speeding puck in his glove.

"Man, how did you ever see that one!" Rusty cried.

"That's goal tending," Pete Tinsley said. "And I mean *goal tending!*"

"He didn't see it!" It was almost a snarl from Cliff Beardsley. "He made a blind stab and came up with a handful of four-leaf clovers!"

68

He caught the speeding puck

Bill eyed the blond boy. "It wasn't so tough," Bill said. "I just figured that you'd shoot instead of passing—puck hog!"

The words surprised Bill a little. Then he thought, he *does* hog the puck. That's the big thing wrong with Beardsley!

"Why, you—you—" Beardsley dropped his stick and lunged toward Bill. "You can't call me a puck hog! I'll—"

"You'll simmer down!"

Coach Le Beau had skated from the boards where he had been watching the scrimmage. Le Beau gripped Beardsley's arm and spun him half around.

"Fighting gets a hockey player nothing but time in the penalty box," the coach said. "All right, that's it for tonight. Squad members will be excused from sixth hour tomorrow. Be dressed and on the ice by the time school is out."

Snow fell heavily when school began the next morning. Boys on the hockey squad were prepared with snow shovels to clear the rink during the noon hour. But there was no letup in the snow. Le Beau called the weather bureau. Indications were that the storm would not abate for another twenty-four hours. Coach Le Beau phoned Falls City and postponed the game.

Northern Tech was playing State that evening,

70

in Northern Tech Ice Palace. The storm would not affect the playing of that game. The Ice Palace was a scant 10 miles from Meinland and trunkline roads were sufficiently cleared of snow to maintain traffic. Bill took a bus to the city.

He looked for a seat at the end of the rink, where he would be able to watch closely the play of goalies. He was surprised to hear his name called.

"Bill Jones! Over here!"

He saw Peggy Sawyer standing and motioning. Terry Sawyer stood beside Peggy.

"Hi," Terry said.

"I phoned your house not five minutes after you'd left," Peggy said. "Daddy had to see Uncle Bert, and he thought you could ride over with us and see the game. You can ride back, anyway."

"It figured you'd be hunting a seat either at this end or the other," Terry said. "They tell me you're going like a whiz in the new job."

Bill was pleased. But he pretended nonchalance.

"So-so," he said. "I've still got things to learn."

"The way I heard you stood off West Fork, I'd say you were learning them pretty well."

Northern Tech warmed up at the end of the rink where Bill and Terry and Peggy sat. Bill studied the Tech goalie. He saw that Terry also studied the man whose job he was slated to take over next season.

"I'm sorry he's a senior, in a way," Terry said. "It'd be something to battle him for the goalie spot. He's a smooth operator. He's got mighty good hands and he uses them!"

Bill nodded. He noted that the Tech goalie made few unnecessary moves. When he did move, he moved fast and surely. It was only a warmup with his own teammates firing the puck at him. But it was the mark of a wise goalie to follow a pattern of conserving energy.

The game began. Bill noticed an odd thing. Terry Sawyer pulled a small notebook from a pocket. He jotted things in the book from time to time. Bill wondered what Terry was doing. Peggy also noticed. She was not as reticent as Bill.

"Whatever are you doing?" she asked. Her dimple flashed. "Don't tell me you're taking notes for a hockey class, Terry!"

"Um-hum." Terry nodded.

"You're fooling!" Peggy studied her cousin. "What are you really doing?"

"Just what you said, taking notes for a hockey class. My own private class. I'm taking notes to add to my book."

Peggy looked at Bill. She said doubtfully, "Is he giving me a line, Bill?"

72

"Don't tell me you're taking notes!"

Bill shrugged. He was as puzzled as Peggy, but he didn't want to expose his ignorance.

"Stop teasing, Terry," Peggy said. "I'm all goose bumps of curiosity."

"I'm not teasing. Tech plays State two games every year and maybe another in a tournament. I just might be the Tech goalie next year. Most of these State guys will be trying to beat me. I'm keeping a book on styles of shooting, tricks they use when they try to deke the goalie, whether they shoot better from right or left, whether they follow any set pattern. Bill knows what I mean, huh, Bill?"

Bill grinned a little sheepishly. There was nothing to be gained by fibbing.

"I probably should have, but I didn't," he admitted. "Do you mean you keep all that stuff on fellows you play against?"

"I've got a book on every guy who's aimed a puck at me in a game for three years," Terry said. "All goalies keep a book. Maybe without knowing it and maybe not in writing. You remember things about players who shoot against you."

Terry grinned.

"Helps you to be on the lookout for things they might do when you play their team again. A former professional goalie wised me it was a smart thing to do when I was a sophomore at Northern High. If you write things down—right after a game when they're fresh—really keep a book, you can go over your book any time and refresh your memory. It helps a lot."

Bill felt a kind of excitement rising in him. He recalled words that Terry Sawyer had said during Christmas vacation . . . "If I can help you, let me know. . . ." Bill looked speculatively at Terry.

"You must have a book on all the shooters in the Border Conference you played against last year," Bill said. "All of them who didn't graduate will be blasting shots at me. How about loaning me your book? You said to let you know if you could help me."

Terry looked startled for a moment. Then a wide grin creased his square face.

"I did, at that," he said. "And I meant it. Peg's dad will be waiting at our place, He won't gripe about waiting a few minutes extra. My stuff on Border Conference players is in another book. I'll give it to you."

"That'll be swell!"

"We goalies have to stick together." Terry chuckled. "There are some pages I'll have to tear out, though. I kept book on fellows on our own team. Wouldn't be right if I gave you dope that would help Meinland trim my old high school. But you'll have the dope on the tricky boys shooting for other Border teams."

Bill nodded. He was grateful to Terry. He was glad that the storm had caused postponement of the Falls City game.

He would study Terry's book on Falls City shooters. He would study the book on shooters of other teams. He would keep a book of his own on boys who had not played last year against Terry.

Hey, this goalkeeping was a pretty complicated business!

CHAPTER 7

Northern High Comes to Meinland

"In case anyone asks you, ten inches of snow is a lot of white stuff to shovel away!"

Dick Carney spoke feelingly. Rusty Hanlon straightened up.

"There is a profound observation if I ever heard one!" he snorted. He put a hand to his back and grimaced. "My aching sacroiliac! I've already shoveled ten *feet* of snow! This shovel handle is just about bent double!"

"That's from leaning on it!" Dick scoffed. "You've hardly made a path wide enough to walk in!"

"We won't get it cleared in time for any practice, if you stand around yakking!" Bill looked up as he pushed a heap of snow past Rusty and Dick. "Let's go!"

"I'm gonna be so pooped I won't be able to skate anyway!" Rusty groaned. "O.K., slave driver!" He leaned into the shovel, dug his skates into the ice and shoved.

Boys on the hockey squad had turned out during noon hour as soon as they had eaten lunch. They had been able to clean but half of the heavy snowfall from the rink. They changed into hockey togs after school and attacked the remainder of the snow. Finally the last narrow ridge was pushed from the rink.

"You'd think fifteen guys could clear this stuff faster than we have," Pete Tinsley said.

"Fourteen, you mean." Walt Pickering inclined his head toward a figure emerging from the door to the dressing room. A flatness that matched his tone was in the gray eyes of the second-line center. "There comes Beardsley."

"I wondered why I hadn't heard him popping off about how they did it back East!"

"He side-stepped the grief," Walt said. "I saw him heading for study hall after sixth hour."

Bill had known that Beardsley was not helping with the clearing job. Beardsley had been conspicuously absent at noon. Bill eyed the blond boy.

"We all turn out when there's shoveling to do," Bill said. "You weren't out here this noon and you wait till the work's done before showing up now!"

"I'm just naturally smart!"

Beardsley grinned. He looked around as

though he expected approval. He met only flat stares and scowls. The grin washed from his face.

"I had to drive my mother downtown this noon," he said. "A teacher gave me a study-hall slip. I couldn't dodge a seventh-hour slip, could I?"

"You could have avoided getting one," Bill said. "Egging a teacher into giving you a seventh-hour slip is an old stunt work dodgers pull."

Beardsley flicked a glance around and then faced Bill.

"Are you saying I deliberately dodged it?"

"You weren't here either time."

"And I told you why. Get off my back, Jones! Maybe a good sock on that loose jaw would tighten it!"

Bill was aware that squad members watched him expectantly. A thought flashed across the back of his mind. I ought to punch him, and I'd enjoy it! But he was captain. Le Beau would take a dim view of his brawling with a teammate. Bill was honest enough to recognize that a large portion of his feeling toward Beardsley stemmed from the fact that the slim blond boy had taken over his job as center of the first line.

"Oh, knock it off!" Bill said. "We aren't a couple of kids with chips on our shoulders. Here comes Coach, anyway."

Coach Le Beau skated onto the rink. He glanced around the group, but his expression gave no indication of whether he was aware of the tension.

"Sorry I'm late," he said. "The principal called me to his office just as I was ready to leave. I'll have to push twice as much snow next time. All right, we'll dispense with play-pattern work tonight. We'll scrimmage until it gets dark. We need to get the kinks out to be ready for Northern."

Twice during that practice scrimmage, Cliff Beardsley beat Bill for goals. The first came on a rebound from a shot that Bill knew he had been lucky to get. He also knew that there is always a certain element of luck in an attacking player's being in exactly the right spot to take advantage of a rebound. He did not mind very much the crack that Beardsley made.

"Well, well, well! I suppose our dream net minder missed that one because he's worn out from shoveling!"

The second time that the slender center beat him, Bill was bothered.

He made a routine glove save of a shot angled at the cage. He turned the puck aside and laid it on the stick of Bert Thomas. The third-string defense man swept around the goal.

Bill thought that Beardsley should have been

back, preparing for defensive play, in position to set up an offensive pattern if a pass should be intercepted. But Beardsley faked Buck Dalton, swept in and poke-checked the disk from Thomas' stick.

Bill was caught flat-footed. Beardsley's whistling drive from the left flashed past and bulged the netting before Bill reacted.

"Just that little four-by-six space to guard, and you go to sleep!" Beardsley jeered as he skated past. "You are tired, Jones!"

Bill gritted his teeth. He had committed the cardinal sin of a goalie. He had allowed his eye to leave the puck because he had anticipated where Beardsley should have been playing. It was salt rubbed into his wound when Coach Le Beau praised Beardsley.

"Alert play," Le Beau said. "Let it be a lesson to you, Thomas. You can't depend on an opponent to fall back because your goalie made a save and handed you the puck."

It was little balm to Bill when Le Beau added, "A clever man on his toes would have made you look bad, Beardsley. I've said a lot of times that hockey is a two-way street. You scored, but you could easily have been left out of the play and put undue pressure on your defense men."

Practice the two days before Northern High came to Meinland rink was rough. Bill wondered if he was imagining it or whether there actually was a rift developing more and more in the play of Meinland's first line. Rusty complained to Dick Carney after the practice immediately preceding the Northern game.

"What are we, stooges for the great Beardsley?" Rusty asked. "It's getting so every time you pass to him, you might as well climb in the stands and watch, as far as expecting a return pass!"

"We're scoring goals. That's what counts."

"Not we—Beardsley!" Rusty scowled. It wasn't like Rusty to scowl. "Man, I'm telling you! It used to be a line when Bill centered us. Now we're a couple of guys named Joe—and Beardsley!"

Northern High came to Meinland sporting a perfect 3–0 record in Border Conference play. Northern enjoyed an advantage over other Conference schools. Northern never had a home game postponed because of a storm. They played their home schedule in Northern Tech Ice Palace. Their boys never had to shovel snow from their rink.

"But that's not going to help them," Rusty said. "This is the year we show the big-city hotshots who's really Conference champs!"

Northern scored a goal at 2:43 of the first period. Le Beau and the Northern coach changed lines

after approximately two minutes, which was standard practice followed by coaches of schoolboy
teams in the Border Conference. It seemed to
Bill that Northern's second line was sharper than
their first line. He had turned back three thrusts
of the first line. He had been particularly watch-
ful of the Northern center. The star almost beat
him in the first twenty seconds. Bill made a mental note to underline in his "book" on this fellow
that he favored a backhand blast after lulling a
goalie into a false security.

The center on the second line was a different
proposition. There was a smoothness, a confidence about his play that was unusual for a high
school player. He roared in at Bill from an angle
the first time. His shot was hard but routine. Bill
smothered it in his pads. A few seconds later,
Walt Pickering's line earned a shot at the Northern goal which was wide. The Northern attacking
line again swept across the Meinland blue line.

He's trying the same thing, Bill thought as he
glued his gaze to the puck. He's coming in just—

That was as far as his thought went. He knew
a second's fraction too late that he had been royally
outsmarted. The Northern center swept his stick
as though shooting. But the puck did not leave
the wood. He skated past the crease, coddling the
black disk in the crook of his stick. He carried the

puck eight feet past the crease before he flicked a sizzling backhander. Bill did not touch the puck.

The same player beat Bill for Northern's second goal a half minute before the end of the first period.

"I've seen that guy somewhere," Beardsley said between periods. "I've played against him, I think. And there was something phony about his eligibility or something."

"You're nuts," Rusty said. "The guy is plenty good. I'll bet he could play with Tech right now and help them. But Northern High has the same eligibility rules we have. They wouldn't be using an ineligible guy."

The tricky center beat Bill for a second time in the middle of the next period. This time Bill was prepared for the maneuver used before. But the center carried the puck past the crease, pivoted in a shower of ice spray, laid a backward pass against the stick of his wing, then pounced on the rebound when Bill sprawled across to block the puck with his stick. The Northern center beat Bill with an easy loft over his sprawling body.

The slick stick-handling star was instrumental in beating Bill for a fourth goal just before the buzzer. It was a wing who blinked the red light. But it was the smooth center who set up the play

84

and forced Bill to commit himself and come out of the crease leaving a wide-open goal.

Northern made the score 5–0 midway of the final period. Again the center of Northern's second line was Bill's nemesis. He snared a loose puck in the neutral zone, flashed a look around and found his wings not in position, and carried the puck in for a solo effort.

It was perfect.

He slipped a check at the blue line. Beardsley was ten yards out of position and the defense man could not take up the slack. The Northern center drove in on Bill alone. Twenty feet out his stick flicked and Bill would have sworn it was a shot. He lunged across the crease to block the puck. At the edge of his vision he caught a blur of motion as the disk sailed unimpeded into the opposite corner.

The scoreboard showed Northern, 5; Meinland 1, after Beardsley finally beat the Northern net minder in the last minute. The same figures were on the board at the game-ending buzzer.

"That guy's been around," Beardsley said in the dressing room. "And he's a phony, some way. If I could just remember where I played against him!"

"Knock it off!" Bill felt as morose as his tone indicated. "They were just better than we were.

That fellow is really good. There's no use trying to alibi!"

He looked at Beardsley. It was in his mind to add something about things maybe being different if a certain fellow played a little more defense. If he would hog the puck a little less frequently.

But there was never much use in trying to alibi.

CHAPTER 8

A Shutout—and a Letter

Falls City High would come to the Meinland rink
Monday to play the postponed game. Friday night
Bill studied the "book" on Falls City boys that
Terry Sawyer had given him. He was up early
Saturday and did his "man-of-the-house" chores.
A letter from Dad came in the mail delivery. Bill
read it eagerly.

> ... Thanks for the newspaper clippings about your
> games. One of the things that I miss most in being
> away from home is seeing you play hockey. Accord-
> ing to the clippings, you're doing a job at goalkeep-
> ing. Stay in there and block those pucks, Bill! ...

The letter gave Bill a tremendous lift. He was
whistling cheerily when he found Mom in the
kitchen.

"I feel so swell I think I'll go for a skate up the
river," Bill said. "Be back before dark."

"I'll never understand it!" Mrs. Jones shook
her head. "You skate when you have something
to think out; you skate when you feel swell!"

Her eyes sparkled as she smiled.

87

"It's a wonder you don't wear ice skates to bed," she said.

Bill stopped at the Sawyers'. Peggy nodded when he asked her if she wanted to go with him.

"I'll get my skates."

There were no skaters in the immediate vicinity when they put on skates at the river bridge, but figures dotted the ice a quarter of a mile or so down the river.

"It's too far to be sure," Bill said. "But that fellow skating near shore might be Rusty. Let's skate downriver instead of up and see."

"It probably is," Peggy said. "Rusty's always trying fancy stops and turns like that."

"Yeah. It helps his hockey play."

The boy skating fast, stopping in a shower of ice snow, then darting in a new direction did prove to be Rusty. Bill and Peggy were fifty or sixty yards away when Rusty abruptly stopped skating. He leaned against an elm tree root that stuck out from the river bank.

"What's with you?" Bill asked.

"I'm practicing."

"We saw you," Peggy said. "You made some fancy turns. You could show me how to do that, sometime."

"I'm getting in practice right now," Rusty said. He was eyeing Bill. "The kind a guy really needs!"

"I'm practicing"

Bill gave him a wary look. A fellow never knew when Rusty was kidding. But Rusty did not give the impression of kidding.

Bill said, "How do you figure leaning against a root is the kind of practice a fellow really needs?"

"It's the next best thing to leaning against rink boards. The way things are, leaning against rink boards is all the practice a guy needs!"

Bill knew what Rusty meant. He also knew that such an attitude was no good.

"When are you going to cut that guy down to size?" Rusty said. "When are you going to butcher our bloated puck hog!"

"I'm not the coach."

"You're captain. Darn it, we've got the stuff to shove Northern out of the championship. Leastwise we *had* the stuff! We had the best production line in the conference when you were centering with me and Dick. That Beardsley! He gets the puck, and the rest of us are supposed to play stooge so he can score! It makes me—oh, heck!"

Rusty abruptly pushed away from the tree root. He skated away, biting his skates into the ice in vicious strokes. Peggy and Bill skated slowly after him. Bill was frowning. After a while Peggy spoke.

"I never saw Rusty worked up before," she said. "He's more than half right, you know."

"There's no 'more than half' about it. Beardsley is a puck hog. He doesn't use his wings the way a center should. He grabs the puck and—"

"That isn't what I mean." Peggy interrupted. "I suppose I see more in a hockey game than most girls. Terry's always pointing out what he calls 'inside stuff' when we go to games. I've noticed that Cliff Beardsley doesn't pass the puck. What I mean is that Rusty is more than half right that you should do something about it."

"I'm not coach! It's not up to me!"

Bill knew that Rusty and Peggy were right. He knew that he should have tried to talk Rusty out of his griping mood. He scowled.

"Knock off the lecture," he said. "Come on, let's skate back."

Bill considered going to Coach le Beau before the Falls City game. But it was Le Beau's fault, wasn't it? He was the wizard who broke up his best line to put a fellow into a job he didn't want, wasn't he? Well, he didn't force you. And you know deep down that you sort of like goalkeeping. So what? It's still up to Le Beau to nail Beardsley's hide to the boards.

Coach Le Beau held his squad in the dressing room for a few minutes before they went out for the Falls City game.

"I've never been much on dressing-room oratory," Le Beau said. "A coach and team must do the basic work in practice. But I admit that this squad puzzles me. We're simply not meshing. You play good hockey in spurts. But a team cannot win playing spotty hockey. Today would be a good time for us to begin to play up to our potential. All right, on the ice. And let's have a little team spirit out there today!

"Beardsley, I'd like you to stay for a minute."

Bill did not learn for some time what Coach Le Beau had to say to Beardsley. He noticed that when the blond center came from the dressing room, there seemed to be a difference in him.

The game began. Almost immediately Bill was called upon to use knowledge that he had gleaned from Terry Sawyer's "book." The left wing of the first Falls City line was their veteran star.

". . . tricky stick-handler. Apt to fool you with sudden burst of speed coming in. Favors shooting ten to fifteen feet out from right side. Cagey. Tries to draw you out of the crease. Carries puck past if you have favorite spot covered. Not a strong shot from left. . . ."

Bill mentally repeated the book as the Falls City star took a pass at the blue line and sped in. The wing stick-handled around Bob Moore's attempted check. Bill crouched. He ignored a shoulder feint, stayed right in the corner of the crease. The Falls City wing swept past the cage mouth without shooting. Bill lined his body and smothered the angled shot that the wing blistered from the left. He dropped the puck to one side of the cage as Rusty swept around the goal.

"Way to go!" Rusty shouted. "No light-blinkers for these jokers today!"

Rusty passed to Dick Carney. Dick flipped the puck to Beardsley. The blond boy set up a play pattern. The Meinland production line swept through the neutral zone. Beardsley laid the puck against Dick's stick an instant before he hit the blue line.

Two fast passes zipped across the ice. Rusty was on the receiving end of the second. He had a stride advantage over the defense man rushing to check him. He had only the goalie to beat.

Rusty blasted the puck—and missed the open corner of the cage by a foot.

Beardsley crowded around the cage. He stole the puck from a Falls City man, bulled free, and centered the puck in front of the goal mouth. A fine setup for Rusty.

Rusty was too anxious. He overskated. Before he could pivot, the goalie leaped from the crease, dropped to the ice, and smothered the puck.

Beardsley skated past Rusty and snarled something. "I suppose you never blew one!" Rusty cried.

That was the closest that Meinland came to scoring during the whole game.

Falls City proved to have very little in the way of attack other than their veteran star. A team that leans too heavily on one man does not do well when that man is stopped. Bill Jones stopped the Falls City ace completely. He made eighteen saves in the game, and fifteen of them were shots aimed by the star.

Meinland forced the Falls City goalie to make twenty-four saves. Some of them were sensational. But the goalkeeper made them. It was a 0–0 score on the board at the final buzzer.

"I knew you'd hang a horse collar on somebody pretty soon," Rusty said to Bill after the game. The usual exuberant bounce was missing from Rusty's tone. "If I hadn't blown those two shots right at the start, we would've murdered them!"

"Must be a great feeling to shut out a team," Pete Tinsley said.

"It's better than the way you feel after a game like that business with Northern," Bill said. "But I'd exchange it for the feeling I had after West Fork. Even if they did beat me once. A shutout is no good when your fellows get shut out, too."

He admitted to himself on the way home that he did feel a glow of satisfaction. Why not? A goalie's job was to keep the other team from scoring. It was up to the offense to beat the other goalie.

This goalkeeping job was all right. The book that Terry had given him helped. And a fellow accumulated dope on opponents who weren't in the book.

Bill felt good. Then he picked up a letter from the table that was addressed to him. The return address on the envelope was Athletic Department, Midstate University. Midstate was a consistent power in collegiate hockey.

Bill's pulse quickened. He ripped open the envelope and read the letter.

Dear Bill Jones:

We are interested in persuading hockey players to attend our university. Boys with scholastic standing to indicate they can maintain collegiate eligibility, and a high school hockey record indicating potential for playing collegiate hockey, particularly appeal to us.

Our material need for forwards should appeal to you. Members of our current first two lines, and the center of our third line, will be lost through graduation.

We have been informed of your record as center of "the finest production line in the Border Conference." We are writing you early to ask that before you decide where you will enroll for your college training, you hear our representative.

We shall have a man in Border Conference territory in late season. Until we see you then, we extend wishes that you may lead your line to a most successful season.

Cordially,
George Farley

Bill stared at the signature. George Farley was hockey coach at Midstate U. He was one of the top hockey coaches in collegiate hockey. Abruptly the warm satisfaction that his shutout had brought drained from Bill.

They wanted centers and wings. They were writing him on the basis of things they knew about his play last year. There wasn't even a hint of any possibility that goalkeeper Jones might be wanted!

CHAPTER 9

This Team of Yours
Has to Jell!

Peggy served a twisting ball that slanted from the table top. Bill's paddle met the ball flatly and took off the spin. His return angled to Peggy's backhand. She was lucky to block the ball. Her return was a weak lob that Bill should have smashed for an easy point.

His paddle swished through the air in a hard swing—and missed the ball entirely. Peggy started a shout of glee, then suddenly broke off. She looked hard at Bill.

"That's the third time you've completely missed the ball," she said. "You're either doing it on purpose or something goony is going on. What's the matter with you?"

"Nothing's the matter."

"You wanted to play table tennis because following the ball would help you follow the puck. You certainly aren't following the ball when you miss like that!"

"So what?" Bill swished his paddle impatiently. "Cut off the gab and serve!"

"What *is* the matter, Bill?"

Bill hesitated.

"It's getting so I feel like I'm using you for confession, or something," he said. "I guess I still need your shoulder to cry on."

"Go ahead—I do it to you lots of times. What's bothering you?"

Bill told her of the letter he had received.

"I try not to kid myself," he finished. "I don't want to take any injured, tramped-down attitude. But just when I've talked myself into accepting the shift Le Beau wanted, and I tell myself that I'm doing what's best for the team and that things will probably work out—well, along comes something like that letter, and I feel like going to Le Beau and throwing my pads and stick at him!"

Peggy said nothing. Bill scowled.

"You may as well spit it out," he growled. "You think I'm being selfish again, like you did when I wasn't going to listen to Le Beau!"

"Boys certainly are funny!" Peggy sighed. "You must feel guilty or you wouldn't think like that. Are you ready for me to serve?"

"Let's call it that you won and knock it off. Right now I don't know whether I'm interested in developing a habit pattern of watching the puck. And it's for sure I don't care enough about this goofy game to play it for fun!"

Tuesday's practice was not a good one. Bill said hardly a word all through the session. He did not notice that Coach Le Beau eyed him at the close of practice. He did not see the worried expression that held the round face of the coach. He dressed quickly and left the rink without waiting for Rusty as he usually did.

Wednesday practice was no improvement. Again Bill spoke very little. Rusty skated beside him off the ice.

"What's the matter with us?" Rusty asked. "It's been like walking around in a cemetery the last couple of days. Are you sore at me for griping about Beardsley, Bill?"

"I'm not sore at anyone. At least I'm not sore at any of the fellows. Maybe I'm disgusted with a lug named Bill Jones!"

"I don't know," Rusty said. "But this team better begin to jell pretty soon!"

Bill saw Terry Sawyer when the Northern Tech Frosh goalie took a seat in the stands near the end of the rink. He wondered idly what Terry was doing at the Meinland rink.

He didn't really think much about why Terry

was there. His thoughts were mostly on the words of Coach Le Beau before the squad went on the ice for practice.

"This is the first squad I've ever coached that has me completely baffled," Le Beau said. "If it's my fault, I want to do whatever should be done. If it's you boys, I'd like you each to figure out what he can do. The main thing is that we have the potential to be a fine hockey team. We haven't approached that potential.

"We go to East Fork Friday and that completes half of our Conference schedule. We're at a crossroads. If we come up to the hockey that we are capable of playing, we can take East Fork. We can go on and give any team in the Border Conference a rough time. But this team has to jell—and quickly!"

There was little indication of any jelling process during that practice.

Coach Le Beau whistled an end to the practice. He skated from the ice with head down. Terry Sawyer leaned over the boards at the curve of the rink as Bill left the goal cage.

"Hi," Terry said.

"Hi. Aren't the Tech Frosh practicing any more?"

"Not this afternoon. The annual Varsity-Frosh game has been moved up to tonight."

100

Terry Sawyer leaned over the boards

"How come you're over here?"

"Thought I'd have a look at how you're doing." Terry grinned easily. "After all, a guy has to look after his protégé. You get any help from the book?"

Bill nodded. He said, "Probably you've been talking with Peggy. Is that it?"

"She mentioned something over the phone about your being pretty low." Terry shrugged. "Guess there's no use in putting on an act. Peg said you'd had a letter and were considering throwing up the goalie job. Don't get things wrong, Bill. Peg doesn't want to interfere in your affairs. It's just that she's mighty concerned that your team doesn't—"

"Okay, okay!" Bill's tone held irritation. "You don't have to build a Federal case!"

"Look, Bill, I don't want to interfere either. Remember you reminded me that I offered any help I could give you? If you still feel you want it, I'll level with you on a few things. If you'd rather, I'll keep out of a thing that doesn't mean any skin off my nose one way or the other."

Bill looked at the older boy a long moment. "I'm sorry," he said. "It sure looks as though we need something. We're coming apart at the seams!"

"A good share of it comes right back to you, Bill."

"Back to me! How? I gave up the place I really want to play, the job I could do. I shut out Falls City. I—"

"It isn't your mechanical play." Terry interrupted. "Maybe I shouldn't judge from watching a half-hour practice. But for what it's worth, here's the way I see it. You can pull your team together simply by taking charge."

Bill jerked his eyes to Terry. He wasn't sure that he followed the Tech Frosh goalie.

"You have the physical equipment for a goalie and you've learned fast. Your technique has improved tremendously since I saw you in the nets at Christmas time. But there's a lot more to being a good goalie than mechanical stuff. Bluntly, Bill, your attitude isn't too good."

Bill bristled. It was on the tip of his tongue to tell Terry Sawyer he was crazy. He bit back his anger.

"You're talking out of both sides of your mouth," he said. "What's wrong with my attitude?"

"A goalie has to be a take-charge guy. A 'holler' guy. He's like a catcher in baseball or a safety man in football. Most of the time the play is in front of

103

him. He shouldn't hesitate to yell to teammates if he sees they're out of position or if a man on the other team is free. A goalie can keep his team hustling by yelling at them. Big-league goalkeepers chatter all the time."

Terry stopped. He looked at Bill.

"You didn't say a word during the part of your practice I saw," Terry said. "If you're going to quit the goalie job, just forget all that I've said. But I don't think you're put together the way a guy'd have to be to quit a thing."

The Tech Frosh goalie put a hand on Bill's shoulder.

"I've ladled out a lot of stuff," Terry said. "Most of it I've just passed on from stuff that was ladled out to me. I told you a former pro goalie sort of took me under his wing the first year I played in high school. Actually, of course, I'm probably stepping out of line. I hope you take things the way I mean them. The thing is, this team of yours has to jell!"

"Rusty and Le Beau and now you." Bill grunted. "So it has to jell and, according to you, I'm the one who has to jell it. Okay, I don't think I'm taking anything you said the wrong way. The question is what to do about it!"

CHAPTER 10

Coach Le Beau Wonders

FORKERS JAB LOCAL SEXTET
East Fork, 6; Meinland, 4

Bill stared morosely at the two lines of type across the top of the sport sheet account of yesterday's game. He had read the piece three times. Now he read it again.

Meinland High completed the first half of its Border Conference schedule Friday with a visit to the East Fork High rink. It would have been better if Coach Le Beau and his squad had "stood in bed." The Forkers handed Meinland its second defeat in Conference play.

Two wins, two losses, and one tie is 'way out of line with the challenger's spot accorded Meinland in preseason dope.

We have followed high school hockey enough years to know that the only predictable thing about a high school hockey squad is that it is entirely unpredictable. So we should not be too critical of our local squad. Suffice it to say that what seemed to be material for a team that would be a real contender in the Border Conference has apparently come unglued.

Nothing went right for Meinland at East Fork. Everything that the Forkers did seemed destined for success.

105

Captain Bill Jones made thirty-four saves in the Meinland cage. Many of them were sensational. Add the six shots that beat Jones and you get an idea of the busy afternoon put in by the Meinland netminder. East Fork's defense allowed Meinland a total of nineteen shots on their goal. That our local lads cashed four of the nineteen—a higher percentage than the Forkers, incidentally—was due largely to the three light-blinkers from the stick of Cliff Beardsley. The smooth-skating center of Le Beau's top line pulled the "hat trick" for the second time this season.

Pete Tinsley, goalie-converted-to-defense man, counted the other Meinland marker. The goal came late in the third period. A booming shot by Beardsley hit the post of the goal cage and Tinsley poked the disk past the goalie.

Your correspondent is well aware that any hockey team may come up with a bad game now and then. Meinland fans can cling to the belief that the East Fork game was merely a bad day for our local sexet. But one or two more games like this and any chance for a respectable finish in the final Border Conference standings will have disappeared.

Coach Le Beau and Captain Bill Jones had better do something to pull the Meinland High team together.

Bill threw the paper to the floor. He sat scowling. That sports writer had rocks in his head! Where did he get that stuff about Captain Bill Jones? He might as well have come right out and blamed a fellow for the sour game.

The doorbell rang. Bill's mother came from a room down the hallway. She was dressed to go out, fastening a scarf around her head.

"Oh, dear," she said. "Your father wrote explicitly that I must deposit the draft he sent no later than today, and the bank closes at noon. I'm such a rattlehead when it comes to business matters! Are you expecting anyone, Bill?"

"I'm not expecting anyone and I don't want to see anyone."

"Good morning, Mrs. Jones." The words came from Coach Le Beau as Bill's mother opened the door. "I'd like to talk with Bill, if he's home."

"He's in the living room. Forgive me, please. I simply have to run!"

"Perfectly all right."

Le Beau came into the living room. Bill was out of the chair and had picked up the newspaper. Le Beau's eyes flicked from the paper to Bill.

"I see you've read it," the coach said. "That's partly why I'm here. Sports writers don't always know what they're writing, I think. But this one has a point in writing that something needs to be done."

Bill scowled. "Why include me? I've gone along with your idea, haven't I? Maybe it would be better if you went back to playing Pete in the nets!"

"I have no complaint about your goalkeeping."

"East Fork beat me six times!"

"And not one of the goals could be charged to faulty goalkeeping."

Bill grunted. Privately he felt the same way. The coach surprised him by taking a letter from his pocket and handing it to him.

"This came in the morning mail," Le Beau said. "Read it."

Bill scanned the letter. "Dear Frenchy: Nice to hear from an old teammate ... appreciate your thought of me in regard to hockey material ... impressed with the record of your boy, Jones. ... Looking for center material ... Jones will have received my letter before now. ..." The signature at the bottom was the same as the signature on the letter that Bill had received.

"That's the main reason I wanted to talk with you," Le Beau said. "This letter didn't sound right. I looked up the carbon of the letter I wrote. I hadn't made it clear that you were not playing center this year, that you'd changed to goalkeeping. I wrote George this morning explaining. I'm sure you'll hear from him further."

"Oh, sure! They want centers and wings. They'll probably beat their brains out to talk to a fellow who was maybe a pretty fair center—but was turned into a pretty poor goalie!"

Coach Le Beau eyed Bill. His round face was sober.

"I guess a man really couldn't expect your resentment to die completely," he said slowly. "I'm going to be blunt. I have no complaint over your goalkeeping. You're a natural in the nets. But you're disappointing as captain. Perhaps it's the resentment. It may be that I pulled a boner. It's late in the season to make changes, but—well, perhaps we'd better make a few."

"It's okay with me." Bill shrugged. He did not intend to let the coach see how deeply he was hurt. "A goalie is a poor spot for a captain. I'll have Mom rip the C off my jersey anytime you say!"

A puzzled expression came over the coach's face. Then he frowned.

"I seem to be unable to say what I mean any better than I write it," he said. "The last thing I want is for you to feel that I'd take away your captaincy. There's nothing wrong with a goalkeeper's being captain. I guess you haven't noticed that since you took over the goalkeeping job, a spot where you're on the ice all the time, I haven't appointed any assistant captains. I was very happy when the boys elected you captain for this season."

Now it was Bill who looked puzzled. He said, "First you say I'm disappointing as captain, that you'd better make some changes. Then you say

109

you were happy that the fellows elected me captain. I don't get it!''

"Wherever you play, you're a natural leader. But you aren't working at it, Bill. Even if you weren't captain, I'd want my goalkeeper to take charge out there. That's what I meant by saying your reaction has been a disappointment. The changes I mentioned include taking you out of the cage. Maybe I'll put Tinsley or some freshman goalkeeping aspirant in there. It's beginning to look as though this season might better be devoted to developing future strength.''

"Now, wait a minute!'' Bill was remembering things that Terry Sawyer had said. "You want your goalie really to take charge out there. You want him to be a holler guy. A goalie has the play in his lap most of the time. If there's some fellow out there fouling things up by hogging the puck, the goalie should cut him down to size. A goalie is really the most important man on the ice for his team.''

Bill stopped. His brow was furrowed, and his features gave every indication that he was immersed in thought.

"In plain, everyday words, it's up to the goalie to keep his team in line,'' he said. "And mow down any character who throws a monkey wrench in the works!''

"Substantially, yes."

"Okay. From now on Bill Jones is going to be captain—and a take-charge guy!"

Le Beau looked speculatively at the captain of his hockey squad. "In the cage?"

Bill looked startled.

"I wonder whether you realize you're putting out pretty strong talk for Bill Jones to continue keeping goal. What about the resentment? What about the letter?"

Bill shifted his weight from one foot to the other. It came to him abruptly with surprised shock that he *wanted* to continue keeping goal.

"Okay," he said. "Maybe a fellow can change. Just forget the letter. I'll forget the resentment."

Coach Le Beau nodded. "Then we have no problem," he said. "But I wonder if you can. I told you I was going to be blunt. I just wonder."

CHAPTER 11

Scrambled Standings

It was not as simple as Bill had thought. Resentment had been too strong in him to forget it just like that. In the first practice for the second Morall game the old feeling welled in him as he watched Cliff Beardsley hogging the puck. Why couldn't Beardsley use Rusty and Dick as a center should use his wings?

Beardsley lost the puck when two defense men sandwich-checked him. The second team swept over the blue line and charged in on Bill.

"Get back!" Bill yelled at Beardsley. "Get in the game!"

The slender center was well out of the play, trailing the attacking line. Bill ignored a feint as a second-team boy skated in. He blocked a hard shot, smothered the puck between pads and glove. Beardsley skated fast around the cage. He was the logical man for Bill to turn the puck to. Instead, Bill risked being called for holding the puck more than three seconds. He slid across the crease.

"Rusty!" he yelled. He dropped the puck to

the ice beside the goal cage. "Take it down, Rusty!"

Rusty snaked the black disk in the crook of his stick. He circled the cage. Beardsley was in poor position to receive a pass but he yelled, "Here! Here! Pass it!"

Rusty ignored the cry. He flipped the puck to Dick. The two wings shuttled the puck between them through the neutral zone. But Dick was a fraction offside at the blue line, and Coach Le Beau shrilled his whistle. Beardsley skated past Bill toward the faceoff spot.

"What's the big idea? I was in better shape to start a play than Hanlon!"

"Right." Bill nodded. "I just thought Rusty and Dick had a right to feel the puck once in a while!"

"Still on me, huh?" Beardsley scowled as he skated to the faceoff circle.

Bill really "took charge" during that practice. He kept up a running fire of chatter.

"Ride him off, Bob! . . . Watch it, Dick, Gus is in the clear! . . . Back, back! He's on your tail, Walt! . . . Pass the puck, Beardsley. Pass it! . . ."

He yelled more at Beardsley to pass than to any other player. At the close of practice, the blond center skated beside Bill.

"You were on me all day," he said. "I don't like

113

it! I score more goals than your pals together! Get off my back!"

Bill eyed the other boy a moment. When he spoke, Bill's tone was level.

"Let's understand a couple of things," he said. "I'm captain. Maybe I haven't really been captain, but from now on I intend to be. I'm not on your back any more than I'll be on Rusty or Dick or anyone else I figure needs it. Sure you've scored more than Rusty and Dick—because you hog the puck and don't give them chances they should have. Don't forget I played center. I know how wings should be used."

"Yeah! That's what's the matter with you. Nobody but Jones ever played center! You're a sorehead, that's all. You don't go for me because I beat you out of centering the top line! Well, I don't go for you either. I'm warning you, lay off!"

Bill said no more. He thought a lot about the charge that Beardsley made. But he did not "lay off." He kept right on yelling. Rusty grinned at his friend at the close of the final practice session before the squad would go to Morall High's rink.

"It's sure good to have you alive out there again," Rusty enthused. "Man, I'm telling you! You're beginning to make this team jell, Bill!"

Morall High played on an outdoor rink. Several inches of snow dropped on the rink the morn-

114

ing of the game and the hurried job Morall boys did clearing the ice was not too good.

"I'm telling you this is really slow ice for skating," Rusty observed during warmup. "But it'll take more than slow ice to slow us today!"

Meinland started in as though determined to make Rusty a good prophet. Beardsley outwhacked the Morall center at the opening faceoff. Dick Carney pounced on the puck. He whizzed a pass to Rusty. Rusty executed one of his patented fancy turns around a check and carried the puck over the blue line. Cliff Beardsley speeding diagonally behind Rusty, yelled, "Down the middle!"

Rusty banged the puck against the boards, pivoted around his check, and picked up the disk. He flicked a perfectly timed pass across the ice as Beardsley drove in. Beardsley's ankle-high shot whizzed past the Morall goalie.

"Man, I'm telling you!" Rusty shouted. "It'll be a breeze!"

It was not a breeze. There could be no doubt that Meinland's play was sharp. But Morall's green team had improved. And the slow ice hampered both teams. On more than one occasion, Le Beau's lines swept into the attacking zone only to lose the puck on underskated passes. Bill kept up a running chatter in the nets.

"Slow it down, slow it down! . . . Cover the wing, Gus. He's in the clear! . . . Back-check, Beardsley, back-check! . . . Watch it, watch it, don't let him pivot! . . . Pass it, pass it, you're too far out to shoot! . . . Close in toward the boards, he's going around you! . . . Get out of there! Stop waving your stick!"

The last was directed at Beardsley. The center had charged in from the side of a Morall wing. He poked his stick as the wing shot. Bill momentarily lost sight of the puck. Luckily the shot was wide. He yelled sharply at Beardsley.

"Stay out of there when you don't have a chance to keep the shot from being made. You wave your stick at the puck and a fellow loses sight of it. And you're liable to deflect a wide shot right into the cage!"

"Make up your mind, Big Stuff!" Beardsley glared. "First you yell at a guy to back-check then beef when he tries it!"

"There's a difference between back-checking and just waving your stick!"

At the buzzer ending the first period the score was Meinland, 1; Morall, 0. Coach Le Beau talked quietly to his squad.

"You played good hockey," he said. "Defensive play was above par. Just one or two things. Let's fire that puck! Keep firing. The more you

116

fire the puck, the more chance you have of scoring goals.

"Rusty, you're checking perfectly until they're across the blue line. Then you're skating in too fast. They slow a little and you're caught for backward passes. All of you remember to keep firing that puck!"

Beardsley looked challengingly at Bill as the teams skated on the ice for the second period.

"Did you hear Coach?" Beardsley said. "He wants us to fire the puck. Keep your eye on me this period, Big Stuff!"

Beardsley scored Meinland's second goal at 1:53 of the second period. He picked up a loose puck at the blue line. Rusty and Dick skated hard on the wings. A Morall boy was fooled by a shoulder feint and Beardsley roared in unchecked on the goal. His blistering shot ricocheted off the goalie's pads. The rebound eluded the goalie's glove and the disk spun crazily in the crease. Beardsley poked it across the red goal line.

Walt Pickering's line cashed a third Meinland goal halfway through the third period. Bill turned back three Morall thrusts. A thought crossed the back of his mind: I've got a shutout going.

He told himself sternly to forget anything like that. The main thing is to keep Morall from getting enough goals to tie or win.

Fifty-two seconds of play remained when Morall rushed in on Bill again. Bill did a split to stop a blazing shot. He caught the blur of a crimson-and-white jersey speeding in from the side. He hurriedly brushed the puck from the crease in front of the Meinland boy. It was Cliff Beardsley.

Beardsley nestled the disk against the blade of his stick. He circled the cage, picked up speed, and used a board carom to evade a check. He picked up the puck and dashed through the neutral zone.

"Pass it!" Bill yelled. "Across to Rusty!"

Beardsley did not pass. He tried to bull through two converging Morall boys. They hit him with simultaneous body checks, and the puck jarred free of his stick. A Morall boy hooked the disk with his stick. He pivoted and dug his skates into the ice. Beardsley jabbed his stick across the Morall boy's middle, and the referee immediately shrilled his whistle.

"Cross-checking," the official called. He jerked a thumb toward the penalty box. "Two-minute penalty!"

"Cross-checking!" Beardsley bellowed. He charged toward the official. "How about those guys both ramming me!"

Captain Bill Jones skated down ice, grabbed Beardsley's shoulder, and spun him around.

"Knock it off," Bill said shortly. "You know it's legal to double-check a man trying to bull through. And jabbing your stick across a fellow's body with no part of the stick on the ice is cross-checking!"

"Listen to Big Stuff who's going to be captain!" Beardsley sneered. "Where I came from, a captain stands up for his men!"

"Knock it off and get in the box!"

Morall's coach pulled a defense man off the ice and replaced him with a forward. Morall grabbed the puck at the faceoff following Beardsley's foul. They swept a power drive in at Bill. Bob Moore and Harry Burns gave ground, attempted to stall the power play. Rusty and Dick harassed wings. But Morall had the extra man.

They beat Bill.

The goal came off a rebound after he stopped a sizzling shot that hit a rough spot in the crease. The rebound was off the edge of Bill's pads. He could not get his glove over in time to smother the puck. The buzzer sounded seconds later.

Meinland, 3; Morall, 1.

Bill gave himself a pep talk. The Morall goal was meaningless. Sure, it was meaningless as far as winning or losing the game. But a fellow had a shutout and then a puck-hogging, shoot-happy slob had to—hold it, Jones! Main thing is for your team to score more goals than the other fellows.

119

Beardsley scored two. Oh, sure! But he had to try for the "hat trick." He could have passed off to Rusty. He *should* have passed off to Rusty. They should have frozen the puck with only seconds to play. There was no excuse for a fellow to cross-check after he was caught in a—oh, knock it off!

Bill swallowed his disgust. Then in the dressing room a thing came up that carried him with the other boys on a flood of excitement of what might be.

"I'm telling you, man, I heard the ref talking to the goal judge," Rusty said. "Don't know whether it was him or not, but some official working Northern's game last week recognized the guy. That joker who played such slick hockey against us for Northern is a ringer!"

"You're crazy! Northern doesn't need ringers. They wouldn't play an ineligible guy!"

"This joker gave them false credentials. He flunked out last year at Forest Academy. He...."

"That's where I saw him!" Cliff Beardsley cut through Rusty's words. "He was Forest's star when they beat us the first game last year. He didn't play the second game because he'd flunked midyear exams. I knew I'd seen him somewhere!"

"What'll they do about it?"

"Northern will have to forfeit all Conference games the guy played in."

"That'll be two losses for them. The trimming they handed us will count as our win. So as of now, we have four wins, one loss, and one tie. Man, I'm telling you! That ought to put us at the head of the Conference standings!"

"Take it easy," Bill said. But his tone held almost as much excitement as Rusty's. "It may turn out to be a false alarm. I just can't see how Northern could slip up. We'd better take it easy till we know for sure."

"One thing for sure: there's going to be a scrambled Conference standing if it turns out that joker *is* ineligible—with us scrambled right up to the top!"

CHAPTER 12

Showdown

Snow fell most of the weekend. The Meinland rink was choked with snow when the boys came with shovels and scrapers Monday during lunch hour.

"Look at all that white stuff!" Rusty sighed. "I'm gonna ask my folks to move to Florida!"

"Then you could play hockey on ponies. Polo, they call it."

"I know what polo is, joker! Saw part of a match on TV. But I thought it was in Texas. Do they play polo in Florida?"

"That match was between a Texas team and a Florida team played at Boca Raton, Florida—I think. I wouldn't know for sure. The farthest south I've ever been is South Avenue in Falls City!"

"Well, anyway, I've got a notion to go over to the airport and hitch a ride to this Boca-what-you-said place. They wouldn't have snow. I've got a notion to—"

"We'd all better get a notion to pile into this snow," Bill interrupted Rusty. "You're giving off the wrong kind of hot air to melt it!   Let's go!"

"Okay, okay!" Rusty grinned.   "There was a show about Uncle Tom's Cabin on that same TV program.   Man, I'm telling you!   You could play Simon Legree on TV!"

The boys attacked the blanket of snow.   Bill glanced around the rink as he returned from shoving a scraper full of snow to the side.   He frowned, looked again.

Everybody was there except Cliff Beardsley and Coach.

They cleared almost half of the rink before they had to leave for afternoon classes.   Bill was in Le Beau's human-behavior class which met fifth hour. Cliff Beardsley was also in that class.   Bill waited in the hall well before the warning buzzer.   The blond boy sauntered down the hall, glanced at Bill, and started toward the classroom door.

"Hold it a minute," Bill said.   "There was snow to shovel today and you dodged it again.   You had to drive your mother downtown.   Right?"

"Wrong!" Beardsley grinned.   His voice held a lazy challenge.   "I had to drive my old man downtown!"

"Knock off the supposed-to-be-funny stuff! You dodged it the other time and you dodged it to-day!"

"I told you I'm sick of your riding me, Jones!

Get off my back, I'm telling you! If you don't, I'll—"

"The assignment sheet is posted on the bulletin board."

Beardsley was interrupted by the words from Le Beau. The coach stood in the doorway talking to a tall woman with gray-flecked brown hair.

"The class knows they'll find tomorrow's assignments there. I've left notes for today's discussion on the desk. I'm sure you will have no trouble, Miss Manley. And I want to tell you how much I appreciate your giving up your free hour to take my class. Maybe there'll come a time when I can return the favor."

"Of course." The woman teacher nodded. "I hope you'll find the roads to the city have been cleared."

Le Beau turned. He saw Bill.

"They've called a meeting of Conference coaches and principals at Northern High this afternoon," the coach said. "I suspect it has to do with charges that Northern has been playing an ineligible boy."

A smile wrinkled Le Beau's round face for a moment.

"Sort of looks as though I have mighty convenient meetings to miss shoveling snow. Tell the boys that I'll shovel while they watch the next time.

I'll get back as soon as possible, but it may be too late for any practice. You're in charge, Bill."

Bill nodded. He watched the coach stride briskly away. He turned again to Beardsley, but the buzzer sounded warning that classtime was only a minute away.

"We'll all be over there after school," Bill said. "With snow shovels!"

Bill had never been enrolled in a class taught by Miss Manley. She taught French and Latin, but Spanish had been his choice for foreign-language requirement. But the word about teachers gets around the student body in any school. Miss Manley was a graduate of an Eastern university. Her broad A's were a bit strange to Meinland boys and girls. But it was unwise to try to be humorous about her "Harvard accent." And she stood for no monkey business.

No one attempted humor or monkey business during discussion of the day's assignment. The class hour was nearly over when Miss Manley summed up the discussion.

"It is recognized that human behavior is the sum total of past experience," she said. "Remnants of culture of every age carry over into future ages. We hear the age of today referred to as the Atomic Age. An age of fabulous—one might say,

125

fantastic—promise. But we must concede that culture and behavior in the Atomic Age must necessarily embody experience gleaned from previous ages of mankind. Even the Dark Ages contributed much to human behavior."

The teacher's broad A made "Dark" sound like "dock." Whether the teacher intended to continue in similar vein, the students never knew. Miss Manley stopped speaking momentarily, and in the interval Cliff Beardsley raised his hand.

"Yes, Mr. Beardsley? You have a question?"

Beardsley looked around, and something in his expression gave Bill a hunch that he was pulling a fast one.

"I was wondering," Beardsley said, "if the dock strikes and unrest we have today came down from the 'Dock Ages'!"

Somebody in a back row tittered, then choked it off as though he had swallowed his tongue. A dead silence fell over the classroom. Miss Manley eyed Beardsley for what seemed minutes.

"There are several connotations of the word 'dock' in addition to a pier or place at which to tie a ship," she said finally. "It may refer to a troublesome weed. Shortcomings may result in one's receiving a dock in reward. One may refer to a place of judgment as a dock.

"Connotation of noxious weed, shortcomings,

a place of judgment, Mr. Beardsley. Perhaps a pun —a feeble play on words—would receive a judgment of noxious shortcoming in the dock of humor. Perhaps a misplaced attempt to inveigle a teacher into meting out a seventh-hour slip would merit a judgment of noxious shortcoming. I doubt that the 'Dock Ages' can be entirely blamed. Do you consider your question answered, Mr. Beardsley?"

The face of the blond boy flushed a dull red. He flicked a quick look at the teacher then dropped his gaze. "Yes'm," he mumbled.

Why, she nailed it right on the head, Bill thought. Beardsley was trying to wiggle a seventh-hour slip to get out of shoveling!

Walt Pickering confirmed Bill's thought as he and Rusty and Bill walked to the rink after school.

"That Manley gal has plenty on the ball," Walt said. "Beardsley asked for it. He must have worked her for a seventh-hour slip the other time there was shoveling to do. I remember I saw him coming from her room heading for study hall that night. Manley's no dope. She had him pegged all the way when he pulled that lousy pun today!"

"And I claim it was really lousy!" Rusty shook his head. "But it sure was funny to watch him stand there and sizzle while she skinned him!"

Beardsley showed up at the rink. And he began feeling the jab of needling from other boys right off. Cracks about dock and noxious and puns that backfired beat around his ears. Bill was surprised at the way the slender center took the razzing.

You have to give him credit, Bill thought. He's smart to see that he'd make things worse by getting sore.

The rink was cleared except for a strip at the curve of the boards at one end when Rusty feigned surprise and pointed at a stick that had been blown into the rink and showed above the snow.

"There won't be any more white stuff to shovel!" Rusty cried. "Spring is here. That's a dock shooting up or I don't know my noxious weeds!"

"You're shortcomings are showing!" Walt Pickering grinned. "That's not a dock. That's the tip of a spear left over from the 'Dock Ages'!"

Bill threw a quick look at Beardsley. The slender boy was trying hard to ignore the cracks. But red flushed up his neck.

"You're both wrong," Bill said. It was the first comment he had made in any way connected with Beardsley's fiasco. "I think it's a piece of a dock of judgment that finally collapsed under the weight of—"

"That does it!" Beardsley threw down his shovel. His face flamed red with anger as he glared at Bill. "I've told you umpteen times to get off my back!"

Bill's amazement at the other's reaction showed in his face. He said, "Take it easy. I was going to say under the weight of cracks that are getting kind of heavy and worn out. You—"

"I know all about what you were going to say!" Beardsley yanked off his mittens. He stood with clenched fists. "I told you before you needed a sock on that loose jaw!"

"Oh, knock it off!" Bill eyed the other boy. "I'm ten pounds heavier than you. My arms are longer. I don't want to fight you or—"

Bill broke off as Beardsley rushed at him, swinging both fists. Bill ducked beneath a wild swing. He knew that he should wrap his arms around Beardsley in a bear hug and hold him until the smaller boy cooled down a bit. But Bill was human. There were things a fellow couldn't take. Beardsley piled into him and a fist caught Bill beneath his ear. The blow stung.

He yanked off his mittens. He was ready when Beardsley rushed again. He swung a balled fist that crunched into Beardsley's chest, and the grunt from the other boy pleased him. They collided with such force that both sprawled on the ice.

An expert observer of the fight would quickly have noted that neither boy knew much about the manly art of self-defense. They knew no more about attack than they knew about defense. They simply barreled into each other and flailed fists.

More blows missed than connected. But every time they collided, the slippery ice did the rest— they both went down.

Suddenly they were threshing in the uncleared snow, fists swinging wildly, with first one then the other on top.

The squad had quickly formed a circle around the battlers. It happened that Bill was on top, spitting and sputtering snow, trying to scramble to his feet, when Coach Le Beau broke through the circle of boys.

The stocky coach wasted no words. He grasped Bill beneath an armpit and heaved. The force of the shove Le Beau gave him nearly upset Bill after he was on his feet. The coach reached down and yanked Beardsley erect.

"That'll be all!" Le Beau's tone was grim. "This had better not happen again, if either of you expects to put on skates for a team of mine again! You young fools! Get—right now! I'm holding every one of you responsible for seeing that there is no more brawling. All of you get out of my sight! I'll shovel the rest of the snow myself! Maybe I can wear off some of the disgust I feel for a gang of high school fellows a man can't leave without coming back and finding them brawling worse than ten-year-old kids!"

They barreled at each other

CHAPTER 13

There May Be Hope

Coach Le Beau gathered his hockey squad along the rink boards near the dressing-room gate. The stocky coach glanced around the group. Bill noted that he was not the only one who dropped his gaze.

All right, he told himself. I've got a good chewing out coming. Let's have it!

He had searched himself pretty thoroughly since the fight with Beardsley. Some of the things he found did not make Bill Jones out as exactly an ideal captain. He was surprised when Le Beau began speaking with no reference to the fight.

"You're all probably wondering about the outcome of yesterday's meeting," the coach said. "Northern High's coach asked their principal to make a thorough investigation a week ago when a referee told him he thought the eligibility of one of his boys was doubtful. There is a strict Conference rule that transfers to any Conference school must meet Conference eligibility standards. A boy must have successfully passed all his subjects the preceding year, as well as maintain passing marks during the semester of competition in any sport.

"The boy in question presented credentials from Forest Academy, which is recognized as having one of the highest scholastic standards in the East. The credentials appeared to be genuine and a clerk in the principal's office accepted them at face value. But when the principal wired Forest Academy, it was learned that the boy had flunked two subjects and had not made up the failures. He had given Northern High credentials arranged to suit himself."

Coach Le Beau stopped a moment, and the suggestion of a smile came to his round face.

"It may surprise some of you who feel that Northern High gets all the breaks to know that it was on a motion of the Northern High principal, seconded by their coach, that Northern forfeited all games in which this boy played."

"Zowie!" the irrepressible Rusty shouted. "That puts us right up there at the top of the league!"

Coach Le Beau nodded.

"The game we lost to Northern goes into our win column," he said. "They also forfeited a game to East Fork. Luckily for them, two of the four games participated in by the ineligible boy were non-Conference games. Northern's Conference record as of now is four victories and two losses. Meinland leads Conference standings with a record of four wins, one loss, and one tie. Since a tie counts as a half-win and half-loss, we're now a half game ahead of Northern."

"Which means that we take the rest of our games and come up to the Northern game only needing to beat those jokers to be champs!" Rusty said.

Again Coach Le Beau nodded.

"That's all," he said dryly. "Just defeat West Fork, Falls City, East Fork, and Northern—and Meinland will win its first Border Conference championship in six years. The question is—can we do it?"

Rusty opened his mouth as though to throw out further exuberance. But something about the expression of the coach stopped him. There was a different quality in Le Beau's tone when he spoke again.

"Now, about the silly thing I found when I came back yesterday," he said. He swiveled a glance from Bill to Beardsley. "Some portion of the blame falls to me. I made a mistake in assuming that I was dealing with high school boys. It may be that I should have tramped on you fellows weeks back. Beardsley, you and I had a talk some time ago. Do you recall what I told you then?"

"Yes, sir."

"Okay. What was it?" the coach insisted.

Beardsley looked up and then down. "You told

me that I wasn't living up to the potential that my skating and stick-handling ability warranted because I apparently had not grown up. You told me that I had to keep in mind that there were other boys on the team besides me.

"You told me"— Beardsley flicked a look at Bill— "that Jones anchored a line much better than I did, but that we needed him as goalkeeper, and I had the potential to come up to his center play."

"All right." Le Beau's tone was a shade grim. "Everything I said still holds. You not only have let your team and your coach down, you've let yourself down. Bill, do you have anything to say?"

Bill squirmed. He had thought that it would be a good thing for him and Beardsley and Coach to have a session of hair-letting-down. But he had not bargained for this public thing.

"Beardsley doesn't use Rusty and Dick the way he should," Bill said. "I'm not moaning any more about playing goalie. I'm a goalkeeper. Period. I have resented Beardsley, and I guess it's showed. I guess I feel different. You have to hand it to a fellow who piles into someone bigger than he is the way Beardsley piled into me. Probably I should have been big enough to have found a way to avoid a fight. I'd like to call it even and start over. But—"

Bill looked steadily at Beardsley.

"I still think a center has to depend on his wings and not hog the puck," he said. "And a fellow has no business dodging his share of work, like snow shoveling!"

Red flushed beneath Beardsley's fair skin.

"I dodged the snow shoveling the first time," he admitted. "But I did have to drive Dad to catch a train the other noon. And it's just plain natural for me to rush that puck when I get it out there. Say that I've been off the beam. Say that it's been worse because Jones had such a big rep and I was trying to beat it. Whether a guy like me can change just like that, I don't know. But I'll sure give it the old college try!"

Le Beau eyed the slender center, shifted his gaze to Bill. The coach's face was sober as he nodded.

"There may be hope for us," he said. "If you fellows mean what you say. All right, let's get rolling and get ready for West Fork."

The week's practice bore fruit when West Fork came to the Meinland rink Friday afternoon. Bill still thought that Beardsley hogged the puck too frequently. But Beardsley scored the first Meinland goal, assisted on a blast that Rusty powered into the nets in the second period, and came up with a solo dash shortly after the two-minute mark of the final twelve minutes for Meinland's third goal. Walt Pickering's line accounted for number four. Bill enjoyed a comparatively easy time in the nets.

West Fork beat him midway of the first period. They beat him again in the closing seconds of the game—on a power play after Gus Schmidt was sent to the penalty box for high-sticking.

The 4–2 win was very satisfactory to Meinland.

"That little clear-the-air session Coach held helped," Rusty said. "Beardsley passed more today. If he gets on the ball and stays there, we're a cinch to come up to the Northern game still leading them."

It was no cinch by any means.

Bill had grave misgivings as the East Fork team warmed up on the Meinland rink two weeks after the West Fork game. Bill was remembering the Falls City game. Beardsley had seemed to be trying hard to overcome his bad habit during the first two periods against Falls City.

Bill had studied his book on Falls City boys. He was confident because of the previous shutout he had handed the downriver boys. It was always an advantage for a team to play on home ice, but Bill believed he could hold off the Falls City attack.

Meinland scored two goals in the first period. And Bill nursed his second-shutout scheme against the Falls City boys well into the third period.

Then Cliff Beardsley broke out in a rash of his old trouble.

He tried to push through the Falls City defense when Dick was in the clear for a pass. He lost the puck. He was left badly out of position as Falls City forwards whizzed through the neutral zone, picked up steam and rolled in on Bill.

Bill managed to save. But he was bothered by the knowledge that there would have been no need for a save if Beardsley hadn't lapsed.

Beardsley made another bad play seconds later. He was outmaneuvered and lost the puck after he had ignored a shout from Bill to pass. He jabbed out his stick in a feeble attempt to harass a Falls City wing. The waving stick made Bill lose sight of the puck for an instant—and that's all it takes. The puck, a shot that would not have been a difficult save, slid past Bill into the corner of the cage.

He glared at Beardsley. Hot words crowded his tongue. But he swallowed them. The game ended with a 2–1 win for Meinland.

"I guess I'll never learn," Beardsley said after the game. "They caught me short. That guy's shot wouldn't have bothered you if I hadn't goofed!"

"Skip it," Bill said shortly. "You overlook a lot of things when you win. Maybe I was slow in getting across to stop it."

Now it was East Fork.

East Fork had lost but two games, both to Northern. One of the losses had been turned into a win because of the eligibility case. A victory over Meinland would tie East Fork with Northern for the lead, with only a game against winless Morall remaining on their schedule.

It boiled down to whether Cliff Beardsley played team hockey or whether—hey, wait a minute! The memory of the 6–4 trimming East Fork had given his team at East Fork was suddenly vivid for Bill! These fellows beat you a half-dozen times! Could be it boils down as much to whether Bill Jones can stop them!

It was a ding-dong battle from the opening face-off. Rusty took a pass from Dick and blasted a sizzling backhander goalward at 8:56 of the first period. East Fork's goalie blocked the shot, but the rebound escaped his clutch. Beardsley slammed the disk into the left lobe of the nets.

"Way to go!" Rusty pounded the center's shoulder. "Way to follow in and fire that puck!"

A minute and twenty seconds later the East Fork center snaked the puck from Beardsley when the Meinland center muffed a chance to pass in the neutral zone. The East Fork boy roared across the blue line, apparently in a solo dash. Bill lined his body with the attacker. But at the last possible

139

instant the center passed off to a wing slanting in from the side. Bill never saw the puck as the center screened for his wing's shot.

Meinland, 1; East Fork, 1. Those figures were on the board at the end of the first period.

It was a rough second period for Bill. He made twelve saves. Seven of them were merely sensational; one was unbelievable. East Fork maintained pressure. Meinland could not get an attack functioning.

"We've got to get going," Bill said as the team skated out for the final period. "A tie will leave us deadlocked with Northern and a half game behind East Fork!"

Walt Pickering's line put pressure on East Fork's defense for two minutes of the third period. Beardsley's line came on. They did not score. Le Beau sent out his third line—Gus Schmidt, Paul Murray, and Bert Thomas.

They had not scored a single goal all season. But they scored a big one at the six-minute point of the third period. Schmidt and Murray collaborated on a fine bit of attack strategy which culminated in Murray's getting a screened shot that whizzed past the goalie unmolested.

"All we gotta do is hold these jokers!" Rusty yelled as the Hanlon-Beardsley-Carney line took the ice. "Pour it to 'em, gang!"

They played good defensive hockey. They made several sashays into East Fork ice but scored no goals. The scoreboard clock ground away time. Meinland's top line skated from the players' box with barely sixty seconds of playing time remaining.

Fifty seconds left. Then forty. Thirty. Fifteen. Ten. Five.

Cliff Beardsley snared a wild East Fork pass in center ice. Bill breathed easier. Rusty was open. Dick was open.

Bill practically jumped up and down in the crease. "Pass it, pass it!" he yelled. "Freeze it! Don't take a chance!"

All that was needed was to keep possession of the puck for a few seconds. But Beardsley barreled through the neutral zone. His stick-handling was flashy. Then all of a sudden it was not flashy. East Fork's center hooked the disk away. Beardsley flung out his stick.

The referee did not blow his whistle, but he held it pointing at Beardsley. A foul with delayed whistle. It would not be called until the attacking team lost the puck. The East Fork center zipped a pass to a wing. The pair rushed at Bill.

Likes to shoot from right side . . . best shot . . . favors it after a fake. . . . Bill's subconscious

141

flashed words from the book Terry Sawyer had given him on East Fork. He glued his gaze to the puck but watched the center from the corner of his vision.

The fake came. Then a whistling, ankle-high shot. Bill crouched in the crease. He felt the shock of the puck against his leg. He dove forward and smothered the rebound just as the game-ending buzzer sounded.

Meinland, 2; East Fork, 1.

"Man, I'm telling you!" Rusty leaped astraddle of Bill and gave him a bear hug. "That's puck grabbing—and I mean *puck grabbing!*"

Bill half pushed Rusty away. He eyed Beardsley as the center skated toward him. It was on the tip of Bill's tongue to read Beardsley off for a crazy thing that had all but cost a tie.

"Okay," Beardsley said. "I pulled a rock. I should have at least frozen that thing. Dish it out, Jones, I've got it coming!"

Suddenly Bill Jones was Captain Bill Jones instead of an irate goalie.

"Let's not go overboard," Bill growled. "We won. You can forget a lot of things when you win!"

"Yes, it may be." The apparently irrelevant words came from Coach Le Beau. He looked from

Bill to Beardsley, and a quirky little smile lifted a corner of his mouth. "It may be that we're finally coming of age," the coach said. "There may be hope!"

CHAPTER 14

Championship Game

Not a single seat was vacant in Northern Tech Ice Palace. One side of the spacious arena held Northern High supporters, the other side held Meinland fans. There was little difference in numbers and no difference discernible in the volume of sound.

Meinland's squad skated onto the ice.

Peggy Sawyer, along with three other girls in crimson skirts and white pullover sweaters with YELL MEINLAND lettered in crimson across the front, leaped and pirouetted as they led a Meinland cheer.

> Shout out the words! Strike up the band!
> Here comes the best team in all the land!
> Meinland! Meinland! Meinland!
> Yea-a-a, *team!*

Bill skated slowly past on the way to the goal cage. He glanced at Peggy. Her dimples flashed.

"Beat 'em, Bill!" she cried. "Beat 'em, beat 'em, beat 'em!"

Terry Sawyer grinned from beneath the stands, where he leaned against the stair wall of a ramp near his cousin.

"Can't desert my high school alma mammy and root for you," Terry said. "But I sure hope you have a good day out there!"

"Thanks. I'd better have a good day! They're a sharp team."

"We're sharper!" Peggy cried. "Terry said a minute ago that a game between two teams as evenly matched as Northern and Meinland is usually decided by play of the goalies. I just know you're the sharpest goalie, Bill!"

Bill looked quickly at Terry. He had thought much in the same vein as Terry. Bill's smile at Peggy was not exactly mirthful.

"I'd like to borrow your confidence," he said.

"It's a good time for all you fellows to play sharp," Terry said. He nodded toward a group of men behind the scorer's table across the rink. "All those men with our coach over there are from different colleges. They're all looking over today's players."

For just a tiny fraction of an instant a twinge of the old resentment ate at Bill. Sure, he thought, and everyone will be watching the scoring lines. Then it was gone. He shrugged.

"I'd settle right now for a win," he said. "Even if I knew no college coach would ever be interested in me."

Both teams played conservative hockey at the

start. It was as though every boy out there recognized that chance-taking hockey was not for a game so important as this one.

Bill shouted encouragement to his team, yelled warnings, kept up a constant chatter.

"Watch that Number 9, Rusty! He's in the clear! . . . Across to Dick, across to Dick! . . . Back-check in there! Worry him! . . . Slow it down, you're charging too fast! . . . Ride him off! . . . Pass it, pass that puck! . . ."

Bill made only four saves during the first twelve minutes. The Northern goalie made but three. None of the seven required more than routine goalie play.

"You played satisfactory hockey," Coach Le Beau told his team between periods. "Be prepared for them to step up the pace next period. Their left side may be vulnerable. The defense man they started is a bit slow in breaking away from the boards. See if we can set up a break-out play on that side."

Northern gained possession of the puck to start the second period. Their coach must have instructed them to try Meinland's right side. Their forwards swarmed into the right half of the neutral zone.

"Watch it!" Bill shouted. "Get across, Bob. They're overloading Harry's zone!"

"Be prepared for them to step up the pace"

Bob Moore did not get across from right defense in time to stop the attack. But he slowed it enough so that by the time a wing slipped Bob's check, he was a little off stride. Bill smothered his shot. He passed the disk off to Rusty as Rusty swung around the cage.

"Set it up," Bill said hurriedly. "The break-out-play!"

Rusty sailed down the right boards. He flipped a pass to Beardsley. Bill yelled, "Set it up!"

Beardsley stick-handled the puck. Dick Hanlon skated toward the left boards. Rusty cut back and behind toward center. Bob Moore and Harry Burns trailed the play, ready to move quickly to defense if the puck should be lost. But Beardsley did not lose it.

He stick-handled away from a poke check. He whizzed a pass back to Bob and broke toward the blue line in center ice. Bob whipped a smooth pass back to the center just short of the blue line. The Northern boy near the boards was forced to move in to check Beardsley—but his move was a bit late and Beardsley flashed over the blue line. Dick and Rusty broke like runaway trains. The out-maneuvered defense man was well taken in by Beardsley's lateral pass to Rusty. Beardsley turned and followed the play quickly. Rusty bored in on goal from the left side.

His shot was hard and on center—but the Northern goalie thrust his wide stick across the cage mouth. The rubber disk banged against the wood. It rebounded, spun lazily 3 feet outside the crease. Momentarily the goalie could not locate it. His frantic dive to smother was too late. Beardsley's following the play paid off. He rapped the puck into the net an instant before the goalie's body would have blocked it.

Meinland, 1; Northern, 0.

Walt Pickering's line came onto the ice. Walt skated past Bill.

"Coach says not to crawl into a shell, but force Northern to take the chances."

Bill nodded. He yelled at his team.

"Easy does it! . . . Make them come to you! . . . Watch that wing, Bob! . . . No, no, no! Make it sure! . . . We can't afford to give them possession on wild passes! . . ."

Bill made five saves that period. But the Meinland defense kept Northern shooters off balance, so that none of the shots was a clear blast. Only one was a fairly tough save. The one-goal margin for Meinland remained when the buzzer ended the second twelve minutes of play.

"A man couldn't ask for better hockey," Coach Le Beau said in the dressing room. "You played sharp, smooth hockey. Maybe we could have

149

broken through once or twice. See if you can set up the same play again. Another goal would be a nice cushion, in case they get lucky and beat Bill."

It seemed to Bill that the Meinland defense suddenly came unglued in the third period. He no more than came up with a save before he was diving across the cage mouth or out of the crease to make another.

If they could just get another goal. A fellow needed a little cushion.

The tempo of the game increased. Meinland geared its play to the tempo. They made it as tough for the Northern goalie as it was for Bill. Time and again the crowd's roar rose as men swept in for shots. Time and again the roar died off in wails and groans. Both goalies were playing tremendous games.

If we could only get another goal! The words pounded in Bill's mind. Northern was called for icing the puck, and he had a chance to glance at the clock before the faceoff. Four minutes and fifteen seconds left.

If they could only score another goal!

Meinland had twice tried to set up the breakout play that had scored for them. Twice it failed. Now they tried it again. The Northern defense man was not slow in leaving the board lane. He broke up the play by intercepting a pass. Northern's attacking line carried the puck out of the defensive zone, across the neutral zone, and rolled in on Bill three strong.

Bob Moore tacked onto a wing. Harry Burns harassed the center. But the other wing got off a shot. Bill's heart leaped into his throat. The puck was flying toward the upper right corner. Bill dove, stretched his gloved hand. He caught the puck. In his relief at making the save, he held the puck overlong. There was a faceoff to the left of Meinland's goal. Both coaches sent out fresh lines.

Buck Dalton snared the puck at the faceoff. He whipped a pass to Pickering. The second-line center stick-handled around a check and sped through the neutral zone. He roared straight in at the goalie. A defense man slanted across to check. Pickering made a fine play. He left a drop pass, drew the defense man to the side.

"Blast it!" Bill yelled. "Beat him, Pete!"

It was not the fault of Pete Tinsley that he did not score. No one could have hit the puck more squarely or with any greater accuracy. It was a wicked, blistering shot 10 inches off the ice and headed for the right corner of the net. And Walt Pickering skated in fast for a possible rebound.

The Northern goalie threw his body across the goal mouth. He went down in a scramble of pads, skates, and sticks as Walt crashed into him. Nobody knew whether the puck was across the goal line. The referee shrilled his whistle. Carefully he disentangled Walt and the goalie. The puck was lodged at the top of one of the goalie's pads—and he was in the crease short of the thin red line.

No goal!

The lines changed shortly after the sensational save. It did not seem to Bill that two minutes had passed. He glanced at the clock. Two minutes and twenty seconds to play.

A lot of things can happen in two minutes and twenty seconds of a hockey game. If they could just score another goal!

Beardsley skated in fast and hooked the puck off the Northern center's stick near the boards. However, he did not get firm possession. The disk skidded free. Both boys lunged for it. Beardsley's shoulder whammed the Northern boy hard. He crashed into the boards, and instantly the referee's whistle blew.

"Charging into the boards!" The official pointed at Beardsley. "Minor penalty!"

"Wh-a-a-t!" Beardsley howled. "I was after the puck!"

Bill skated from the crease. He faced the official.

"I didn't see any foul," Bill said.

The referee explained. Beardsley was as close to hopping up and down as a boy on skates could be. Bill put out a hand to restrain him.

"He's the ref," Bill said. He eyed the official. "But that's calling it pretty close, I'd say!"

"You're entitled to register a protest." The referee shrugged. "If we didn't call 'em close, a game like this could get out of hand mighty quick!"

Beardsley went to the penalty box. Bill glanced at the scoreboard clock. It showed 9:53. Two minutes and seven seconds of playing time left. Beardsley would be in the penalty box for two minutes.

Meinland would be a man short the rest of the game, for all practical purposes.

CHAPTER 15

Two Minutes to Play

Northern's coach sent a forward to replace a defense man. The Meinland defense would have to contend with power play after power play. Dick Hanlon secured the puck at the faceoff. He passed to Rusty. Rusty attempted to stick-handle the disk, control it to kill time. For just an instant Bill wished that he were playing center again. He had been the best penalty killer in the Conference. But Rusty was far from the best. He lost the puck.

Northern poured a four-man drive down ice. Meinland boys back-checked, tried desperately to break up the attack. Harry Burns managed to bump a wing enough so that his shot at Bill lacked steam. Bill smothered the disk. He took as much time as he dared in handing off to Dick at the end of the cage.

"Take it easy," Bill panted. "Stall as much as you can. Every second counts!"

Two Northern boys battled with Dick along the boards behind the cage. Suddenly the puck squirted out, ricocheted from the boards. Bill

154

leaped from his crease. He swept his stick wide and banged the puck as hard as he could toward the Northern end. There is no penalty for icing the puck when your team is shorthanded.

Northern's goalie turned the puck aside to a teammate. Northern gathered their attacking force again. They rolled from the defensive zone across the neutral zone and into Meinland ice. What seemed to him like umpteen men drove in at Bill.

He made a fine save of a waist-high shot. He took his time in handing off the puck.

Three more times Bill staved off power drives. But he knew that he couldn't go on forever. Another Northern forward clambered from the player's box and replaced a defense man. Five forwards on the ice for Northern now.

Bill sneaked a glance at the clock. The second hand swung into the final minute. Then he caught a glimpse of a bulky figure out of the corner of his eye. It was the Northern goalie, skating to the players' box.

Northern's coach was taking a calculated risk. He was pulling his goalie. Now they had a six-man attack. Bill crouched in his crease. He yelled at his mates.

"Cover the side! . . . Watch him down the middle! . . . Bother them! . . .

It's a tough task for four men to cover six attackers. Northern rolled over the blue line. Bill fastened his gaze on the puck. He dared not lose sight of it for an instant. He had to anticipate. Northern's center was their best shot. They would probably maneuver him into . . .

Bill's thoughts broke off. He sensed the shot just before the Northern center's wrists tensed. Bill came out of the crease to lessen the angle. His skates were together, pads close. The puck whammed into his skates. It rebounded fast, past the jabbing stick of a wing.

Afterward Bill wondered what happened to him. It could have been that reflexes he had developed while playing center took charge.

He leaped forward and drove at the puck. He did not fall on the ice to smother it. Northern boys were caught momentarily behind him. Nothing but clear ice loomed between him and the distant Northern wide open goal.

"Rusty!" he yelled. "Dick! We're taking it down!"

He was an awkward figure, encumbered by goalie pads and hampered by slow skates. He glanced frantically to each side. Neither Rusty nor Dick was there.

He thought, It's too far for a shot. If I can get into the neutral zone, I could drill one into that open net. It's too far for accuracy from out here.

A solid body check from the side jarred him. He was knocked sprawling. In the instant that he scrambled to his feet, Bill mentally hurled bitter recrimination at himself. Any dope should have known better!

Northern was a cinch to count the tying goal with no goalkeeper in the net and six forwards. Bill strained desperately to get back. He knew he could never make it in time.

Northern's center had the puck. He tensed to shoot. And suddenly he was knocked to the ice.

Cliff Beardsley had vaulted over the boards of the penalty box. He flung himself at the Northern center. The puck slanted off Beardsley's stick.

Beardsley pawed and clawed and scrambled for the puck. Two Northern boys skated in fast. Bill Jones reached deep into his physical reserve and strained forward with every atom. He threw himself in a lunging dive as a Northern wing shot.

His stick deflected the puck, half stopped it. Bill scrambled over the ice. His glove covered the disk an instant before a Northern stick whammed it. He was barely conscious of the shock of the blow through his padded glove. The main thing was that the puck was beneath the glove. The referee's whistle shrilled.

Now came confusion. A big rhubarb.

157

"He can't cover the puck way out of his crease!
... Beardsley left the box before his penalty was
up! ... He couldn't play the puck like that! ...
We get a penalty shot! ..."

The Northern captain grabbed Beardsley, yelling, "You left the box too soon!"

"You're crazy!" Beardsley jerked free. "Ask
the penalty timekeeper! I didn't leave till he told
me my time was up!"

"Who's crazy? You pulled a fast one! You
won't get away with it! You need a sock in the—"

"Nobody's going to sock him!" Bill spun the
Northern captain around. "If there's any socking
I'm going to be in on it!"

The referee pushed between the two captains.

"Tempers get short in a tough game," the official said. "Take it easy, both of you. We'll do
any checking necessary!"

The officials checked. The penalty timekeeper
assured the referee that there was nothing against
Beardsley.

"He got over the boards faster than I've ever seen
a man get out of the penalty box before," the timekeeper said. "But he didn't budge till I signaled
his penalty time was up."

The referee explained to the Northern captain
that he had no just complaint concerning Bill's
holding the puck.

"Rule 11, Section 7b," the referee quoted. " 'Within the rectangular area bounded in the rear by his end of the rink, in front by an imaginary line connecting the Special Spots, and on the sides by imaginary lines from the Special Spots to the end boards, the Goalkeeper has certain privileges.' "

The official smiled.

"Even if he has been making like a forward," he said. "A goalkeeper can catch or propel or trap or cover the puck to prevent an opponent from scoring."

Exactly three seconds showed on the clock when the rhubarb was settled. Beardsley whacked viciously at the puck when the referee dropped it for a faceoff. He kept whacking at it. He and the Northern center were still clashing sticks, trying to free the disk, when the game-ending buzzer rasped.

Meinland, 1; Northern, 0.

The figures on the scoreboard were lovely. Bill Jones stood in the crease admiring them. He was suddenly lifted bodily. Beardsley and Rusty and Dick and Pete—the whole squad mauled him.

"What a puck grabber! . . . Man, I'm telling you! . . . A shutout in the championship game! How about that! . . .

Bill struggled to his skates. He grinned at Beardsley.

159

"We're even for anything now for sure!" Bill said. "You saved my life stopping that shot!"

Beardsley grinned. "You were doing all right as a puck carrier when you went past the box," he said. "I thought you were going to put something new in the record book—a solo goal by a goalie!"

"That crazy stunt!" Bill grimaced. "I must have been goofy from thinking how swell another goal would be. I had rocks in my head! You saved the game!"

"You did more than a bit of saving yourself—Puck Grabber!"

Cliff Beardsley grinned as he added the "Puck Grabber." His eyes sparkled. And suddenly Bill liked the sound of "Puck Grabber." He grinned back at Beardsley.

Coach Le Beau said, "If the mutual admiration society can call a few minutes' halt, there are several college hockey coaches who would like to talk to you fellows."

Bill looked at the coach. Le Beau's eyes twinkled and a smile wreathed his round face.

"Okay," Bill said. "I'd like to talk to them. That's if any of them wants a"—he winked at Cliff Beardsley, then finished—"if they want a puck grabber!"